Stand Real Still, for Openers...

"Soon as I relieve you of that Colt you're carrying, I'll feel better about taking a closer look at you."

Longarm felt a hand grasp the butt of his revolver and lift it from his holster. He stood motionless, waiting for the man to search him further, but his captor did not bother to look for other weapons.

"Now march on in to where the Kid and Annie can get a look at you," the man ordered.

Before Longarm could move, he heard a crash followed by a scuffing of moccasin-clad feet from the cave. The Apache Kid appeared in the passageway, his own revolver drawn. He glanced at Longarm and his eyes narrowed with hatred...

Also in the LONGARM series
from Jove

→ **TABOR EVANS** ←

LONGARM

AND THE
DESPERATE MANHUNT

A JOVE BOOK

LONGARM AND THE DESPERATE MANHUNT

A Jove Book/published by arrangement with
the author

PRINTING HISTORY
Jove edition/June 1987

ISBN: 0-515-09007-7

Jove Books are published by The Berkley Publishing Group,
200 Madison Avenue, New York, NY 10016.
The words "A JOVE BOOK" and the "J" with sunburst
are trademarks belonging to Jove Publications, Inc.

PRINTED IN THE UNITED STATES OF AMERICA

Chapter 1

It was the wheeling circle of buzzards in the cloudless sky, the only moving objects he had seen all day, that led Longarm to the spot. The big birds stood out sharp and clear, riding the faint updrafts which rose from the sun-baked soil and penetrated through the ground-hugging heat haze. The buzzards were circling with the patience of their kind. Longarm had no doubt about what they were doing. Their habit was to wait patiently, making sure that whatever they were watching on the ground was dead and unable to fight them when they swooped down for their grisly scavenger's feast.

Trails were almost nonexistent in the country Longarm was crossing now. Mile after dreary mile, the landscape looked exactly the same. It was a monotony of pale color, yellow sand, brown and reddish rock outcrops, and huge swatches of pale scrubby gray-green sagebrush. At sunrise the sky had been deep blue, but as the day had worn on its hue faded until it showed even less color than the ground.

Now it was a colorless haze of infinite nothingness. In this kind of country, buzzards meant death, and death meant trou-

1

ble. Though Longarm wasn't in search of either, he reined his horse toward the half-dozen circling birds.

Keeping the buzzards in sight was no trick. Even a tenderfoot could have cut a straight line to them in that part of Nevada. The land was level. The nearest mountains were behind him, while those ahead were only vague, veiled jagged cones, barely visible through the shimmering heat haze. There were no tall trees to obscure the sky, no trails through the low-growing sagebrush which bristled thickly from the tan-colored earth.

From the way the buzzards were acting, circling warily for several minutes above the ground, dipping low for a few minutes now and then, and suddenly gaining altitude to resume their circles, Longarm judged that whatever they were watching was not yet dead, but was very close to dying. He also judged that the buzzards' quarry must be large.

In the distasteful circle of carrion eaters to which the buzzards belonged, there was rarely a pecking fight over food. A small dead animal such as a packrat or a rabbit or even a lean-shanked, long-toothed peccary would have drawn only a single buzzard, certainly not more than two. Only when the prospective feast consisted of an animal carcass such as that of a wild mustang or a steer—or, Longarm thought wryly, a luckless prospector—would it attract as many birds as now swirled through the upper air waiting for their meal to die.

In the flat, featureless country over which he was riding, Longarm could cut a straight line toward the area where the buzzards were circling. He neither dawdled nor hurried, but let his livery horse set its own gait, just a bit faster than a trail walk, as he advanced steadily toward the birds.

His ride lasted longer than he'd anticipated, but he knew that as long as the buzzards stayed aloft there was no need to hurry. They would not swoop down until they were sure that whatever they had sighted dying was completely dead. Many months had passed since Longarm had last been in Nevada Territory, and he had forgotten how deceptive the distances were on the flats that stretched between the small mountain ranges in the central and southern parts of its terrain.

Well, old son, Longarm told himself silently as he fished

2

one of his long thin cigars out of his vest pocket and clamped it between his strong teeth, *looks like whatever them buzzards is waiting for is going to hold out till you get there. Chances are it won't be such a much, though. Likely all you're going to find is one of them wild mustangs that got too old to keep up with the herd, or maybe a crippled burro that some prospector's turned loose to wander off and die. Still, if it is a human being they're after, and he manages to stay alive till you get to him, he'll be awful glad to see you.*

Flicking a match head across his thumbnail, Longarm lighted the cigar and rode on toward the soaring circling buzzards.

Until he got within a quarter of a mile of the spot over which they were soaring, a series of rising hillocks topped with sagebushes hid the ground from view. Then he reached the last of the little rises and could see the ground ahead. His jaw set grimly and his lips compressed into a thin line around his cigar when he saw what remained of a burned-out wagon.

Its wheels with their iron tires had escaped the flames, though the tops of the high rear wheels were badly charred. The wagon stood on a little flat in the center of a rough circle of broken ground. The circle had not been formed by nature, but by the hooves of Indian ponies. The U-shaped marks of pounding hooves were visible in the desert soil even from the distance that still stretched between Longarm and the charred wagonbed.

There were no bodies around the partly destroyed vehicle, no signs of the horses or mules that had drawn it there. The wagon-tongue slanted to the ground, the harness straps and reins had been corkscrewed by the flames and lay tangled on the ground around the tongue. The fire that had consumed the wagon's canvas top and bows and eaten down its sideboards had also burned away the seat, but the arced springs which had supported the seat curved above the charred sides.

From the distance all that Longarm could see were lumps in its low boxlike bed. His lips pressed still more firmly into their thin angry line, Longarm toed the livery horse ahead. The buzzards shrilled with harsh, high-pitched cries and much clacking of their needle-pointed beaks, but they broke their

3

circle and began flapping away. The last of them showed only as a small black dot in the distance by the time Longarm reined up beside the burned vehicle.

Its sideboards, or what remained of them, bore the pocks of bullet-holes, and now he could see clearly that two of the lumps in the wagonbed were corpses. There was no mistaking the outlined shapes, and the rancid smell of human flesh charred by a killing fire hung like an almost visible pall over the scene.

Longarm had both seen and smelled death many times, but the odor of a burned body still gagged him. He did no more than glance at the huddled figures, almost completely concealed by the black curled shards of the canvas top, but turned his attention to the other objects in the wagonbed.

These were almost totally unidentifiable as well, but he could guess at the piles of ash that still bore vague outline and shape. A bit of study enabled him to pick out the ash heaps that had been bedrolls and boxes of clothing and food. The edge of a shovel and the curved head of a pick protruded below what was left of the wagon-seat, and near them a cast-iron pot and skillet and the rims of a few tin plates were sticking out of the rubble that remained.

Shaking his head sadly, Longarm said aloud, "Whoever them two poor devils was didn't have much of a chance, it looks like." Then, between thoughtful puffs of his cheroot, he went on as he studied the ruined wagon, "Easy enough to see what happened, though. Them redskins must've spotted the wagon when it was still a good piece away. They was waiting below that rise yonder, and jumped it when it started across the flat."

Toeing his horse to a walk, Longarm rode slowly in a circle around the devastated wagon. "There ain't no easy way of telling how many Indians there was," he mused aloud, examining the wagon and studying the hoofprints. "And in this country, where it's so dry and all, there ain't much way to figure how long ago the fight was. But the buzzards up there's still waiting for them bodies to get ripe, so it must've been just a day or so ago, maybe as much as three days."

After he'd made another circuit around the wagon, noting

4

the trampled vegetation that encircled it in a wide swathe, he went on, "It's sure as God made little green apples that them folks in the wagon was outnumbered about ten to one. But the two of 'em put up a right good fight. Them scuffed-up places where there's blood caked in the dirt shows they must've knocked three or four redskins off their horses, and judging by the way the ground was tore up by them hoofprints in that circle the redskins' ponies made, they rode around the wagon for quite some time."

Satisfied at last that he'd gotten all the information possible from the tracks around the wagon, Longarm dismounted and prepared to take care of the part of his job that was least pleasant, the part he'd put off as long as possible by making a minute examination of the evidence left around it by the fight.

Climbing into the wagonbed, he took a tin plate that stuck up from the top of one of the badly charred boxes and scraped away the stiff shards of burned canvas that covered the face of the nearest the two corpses. It was a gruesome task. His painstaking efforts uncovered nothing but white bone, and he realized at once that the job he was trying to do was futile. No matter how carefully he approached the grisly job, he would never be able to determine how either of the two bodies had looked in life, or even whether they were the corpses of two men or those of a man and a woman.

"You sure hit a dead end here, old son," Longarm muttered under his breath as he put the tin plate aside and rose to his feet. "They're just burned too bad. So is about everything in the wagon here that'd give you any kind of hint who they might've been, or where they started out from.

"Now, a doctor might be able to tell whether they was both men or whether they was a man and a woman. Trouble is, you ain't no doctor, and there ain't likely to be one just ride up and offer to help you figure things out. The only thing you can do is bury what's left of 'em, and then see if you can track down the sons of bitches that killed 'em."

Stepping back to the wagonseat, Longarm picked up the blade of the shovel. As he lifted it he saw that the handle had burned down to a foot-long stub, and a glance at the pickaxe showed that its handle had burned away completely. With a shrug he stepped to the side of the wagonbed and dropped to the ground, carrying the stub-handled shovel. Looking around, he could see no better place to dig than in the area beside the wagon, so he began lifting out crumbly clods of the sandy soil.

Digging with a shovel that had a handle no more than two feet long proved more of a task than he had anticipated. Though the earth was dry, it was really almost too dry. Half the dirt on the shovel cascaded off the blade before Longarm could lift it to toss it aside. At last he resorted to rabbit-digging, pushing the blade into the sandy soil and scooping it from the hole with short swings of his truncated tool.

That method worked only until he'd gotten a foot or so below the surface, though. Sweat had begun dripping off Longarm's chin almost the instant he had begun to dig. Soon it was pouring down from his chin and the tip of his nose, and he could feel his body growing moist under his longjohns.

Stubborn in his purpose, Longarm kept battling the loose trickling soil with his crippled shovel until he had made a slant-sided square hole almost four feet deep and three feet wide in the stubbornly shifting earth. He had noticed when he first looked into the wagonbed that the feet and lower legs of the two corpses had been almost completely burned away. Scrambling out of the hole, he sought the patch of shade which had begun to stretch away from the east side of the wagon as the sun dropped lower and lower.

He tried without much success to brush away the gritty sand that had accumulated on his sweat-dampened hands, and after getting off all but a film of the tight-holding grains he lifted his canteen out of its saddle-sling and treated his gritty mouth and parched throat to a swallow of warm, brackish water. Then he sat down and leaned back against the rear wheel of the wagon. Taking out a cigar, he lighted it and sat staring across the expanse of green-gray sage and yellow sand as he contemplated the grisly work that still must be done.

There ain't no reason for putting it off any longer, old son, he told himself at last. *You've done the hard part of the work, so you might as well chomp your teeth together and go on with finishing it.*

6

Reluctantly, Longarm unfolded his long legs and stood up. Knowing from past experience how the stench of dead human flesh ripened in the desert sun clung to clothing, he stripped naked, hanging his clothing over what was left of the rear wagon-wheel.

Holding his breath as much as possible, he lifted what remained of the two corpses from the wagonbed. The flames that must have engulfed the wagon had done their work only too well, as had the sun. The flesh on both bodies had already started to soften, and what remained was unwieldy and hard to handle.

At last he had them deposited in the crude trench, and without stopping to rest he shoveled the loose soil back into the little excavation and added more on top of the filled bulge until it was mounded into at least the semblance of a grave. By the time he'd finished the job, perspiration was dripping from Longarm's nose and chin, his fingertips and elbows, and running in swollen drops down his bare legs. In spite of his copious sweating, he was aware that the odor of death was clinging to him.

Hurrying back to the patch of shade on the other side of the wagon, Longarm swallowed a few sips of tepid water from his canteen before folding his trousers into a rough cushion, which he placed beside the wagon-wheel. Stepping to the edge of the shaded area, he scuffed his bare feet in the dry sandy soil until he had loosened an area a yard square, then began scooping up handfuls and rubbing himself down with it.

He worked methodically, scouring his body with firm strokes until the sand had absorbed the perspiration, then rubbing and brushing it off. By the time he had finished and gone over his hands and arms a second and third time, the odor of the grave had almost completely vanished.

His efforts had started him to sweating again, but he had allowed for that. To give himself time to dry, he went back to the wagon and sat down on the cushion he had made of his trousers. His longjohns and shirt were still draped over the burned-out wagon-wheel, his vest and pistol belt beside them. Leaning and stretching, Longarm reached for his vest and took out a fresh cheroot and matches. Lighting up, he let himself relax while waiting for the warm desert air to dry him once more.

He had been sitting puffing his cigar for several minutes, considering his next move, his eyes on the featureless terrain that stretched away from the wagon, when a faint noise reached his ears. The soft rustling sounded like a puff of breeze passing over the sagebrush, and Longarm paid little attention to it. Then the noise was repeated and he listened more carefully. When he heard the same soft rustle of sound for the third time, he was sure it could not possibly be the wind. Clamping his cigar firmly between his teeth, he brought his right hand up slowly to the pistol belt and closed it around the butt of his revolver.

When he heard the sound again, Longarm leaped to his feet, whipping his Colt from its holster as he rose and swivelling in the direction of the noise. As he turned, he leveled the Colt toward the back of the wagon. Then his jaw dropped open in amazement and his eyes widened when he saw a young woman standing behind the wagon staring at him. Her mouth and eyes were opened almost as wide as Longarm's. They stared silently at one another for a moment, then Longarm spoke.

"I guess you ain't learned yet that it's dangerous to sneak up on a man the way you was doing," he said. "But you sorta surprised me, soft-footing up that way."

"I—I'm sorry," she stammered, her voice still strained and her eyes still fixed on Longarm. "But I couldn't see you very well from where I was hiding, and about all I could think of was trying to be sure that I wouldn't make any mistake if I came out of hiding. But I was so thirsty—"

"I guess you are, if you been hiding any length of time," Longarm said.

He covered the distance to his horse in three long steps and came back with his canteen. The woman reached for it instantly, but Longarm kept a firm hold on the round blanket-covered canteen when she tried to take it from him.

"Now, just wait a minute," he said. "If you been without water very long, you don't wanta take big swallows."

8

"I haven't had a drink of water since the day before yesterday," she told him. "Please—"

"Easy does it," Longarm cautioned, keeping a firm grip on the canteen while she struggled to lift it to her lips. He let her put her hands over his and raise the canteen to drink, but when she'd had only two small swallows he pulled it away from her mouth. "Just let me hold this a minute. I'll tilt it up till you get as much as you oughta drink at first."

"But I'm so thirsty!" she pleaded. "Please, I want more!"

Again Longarm kept a tight grip on the container and pulled it away from her mouth after she had swallowed three times.

"Now let what you've had settle down," he cautioned. "And don't worry, I ain't aiming to do nothing but help you. I'm a deputy United States marshal, and my name's Custis Long."

"My name's Sarah Roundtree," she said. "And please, can't I have another drink of water before we talk any more?"

"Sure." Longarm held the canteen to Sarah's mouth again, letting her take four substantial swallows this time before pulling it away. He went on, "Now, that's all you better drink this time. Wait about ten minutes, and you can have some more."

As Longarm pulled the canteen away from Sarah's clutching hands he was aware for the first time of a peculiar expression on her face. He suddenly realized the reason and reached for his pants. Keeping his back to her, he stepped into the trousers quickly and turned back to face her.

"I'm sorry if you was embarrassed by seeing me naked," he apologized. "I took my clothes off when I buried the— your folks, so I wouldn't ... well, they'd been dead long enough so that they—" He stopped short, realizing the clumsiness of what he'd been about to say. Then he went on, "If you don't mind looking the other way for a minute, I'll get dressed proper."

"I'll get out of your way completely," Sarah replied. "While you're dressing, I'll step around to the other side of the wagon. That was my Uncle Frank and Aunt Glory you buried, and I'd like to say a little prayer for them."

"You go right ahead and do that," Longarm nodded. "It'll only take me a minute or so to get decent again. Then we can have a little talk, and you can tell me what happened. Then we better figure out the best thing for you to do."

Chapter 2

Longarm wasted no time when Sarah Roundtree disappeared around the wagon's tailgate. He stepped out of his trousers and brushed his hands over his body to remove the last few grains of sand that still clung to his skin. Then he hurriedly put on his longjohns, shirt, trousers, boots, and vest. When he had buckled on his gunbelt and stamped into his boots, he stepped around the end of the wagon. Sarah was on her knees beside the crude grave, her head bowed and her eyes closed.

She had not seen or heard Longarm approach, and he stood silently at the corner of the wagonbed, getting his first good look at her.

At some time after Sarah had gotten out of his sight she had smoothed her tangled dark blond hair and knotted a short length of leather thong around it at the nape of her neck. Now it fell in a loose fanlike spread down the back of her checked gingham dress. Even though she was kneeling, Longarm could notice details of her appearance that had escaped him earlier. Sarah was tall, and had a full figure. He also noticed with some surprise that Sarah was older than he'd taken her to be at his first hurried and embarrassed glance, and though her eyes were now closed he remembered that they were a light blue. Her cheekbones were high, almost Indian-high, and her nose was a short, straight line that ended in flaring nostrils. Her lips were full and her chin firm, and though her hands were folded below her bent head he could see that their backs bore the stamp of hard work.

Longarm stood silently watching until Sarah finished her prayer and she did not see him until she rose to her feet.

"It was thoughtful of you to bury Uncle Frank and Aunt Glory," she said. "I haven't thanked you yet, but I am grateful to you for taking care of them. Now, could I please have another drink of water?"

"Why, sure. You can take three or four big swallows now, but was I you, I wouldn't drink any more till later on. I'd bet you're pretty hungry, too. Let's go back to the shady side of the wagon while you tell me about what happened. I'll have to put in a report on it, you know."

"I hadn't thought about that," Sarah said as she walked beside Longarm while they returned to the only patch of shade visible anywhere in the flat, sun-bathed landscape. "But there's really not much to tell."

"From what I saw, I figured you and your folks had just pulled up here on the flat when the redskins jumped you," he said.

"Yes. It was the day before yesterday. Uncle Frank stopped the team and said we'd better stay here on the flat overnight, even if there wasn't any water close by. He mentioned being afraid the water keg was getting pretty low. He was right, too. I saw it burning when the Indians set fire to the wagon."

Longarm picked up his canteen and handed it to Sarah. "Not more'n three or four swallows, now," he told her.

She took four large but carefully calculated swallows of the tepid water, then capped the canteen and handed it to Longarm.

"I'll take your advice, Marshal Long, because it's been very good so far," she told him. "And I still haven't really apologized for startling you when I came up to the wagon a while ago. I'm sorry, but I was just trying to be careful."

12

"Being careful ain't always the best thing," he told her. "It just about got you shot."

"I said I was sorry," she reminded him. "The trouble was that I could only get a glimpse of you through the sagebrush, and I was afraid the Indians might've come back."

"You was in the wagon when they jumped it?" Longarm asked. When she nodded silently, he went on, "I'm sorry I didn't get here in time to help you and your folks stand off them redskins."

"That's not your fault," Sarah said quickly. "And I do understand why you buried them as soon as you could. I know about the smell of death. It's just that I was surprised when I saw that you didn't have any clothes on. But it was sensible to take them off."

"I couldn't figure out what else to do," Longarm nodded. "There's not much telling when a man'll get a chance to have his clothes washed out here on the desert. Course, I didn't have no way of knowing you was out there in the sagebrush."

"I'm sure it wasn't a very pleasant job," she went on. "And I sort of shiver when I think that if Uncle Frank hadn't told Glory and me to run and hide, you might have had to dig a grave big enough for all three of us."

"I been wondering how you happened to get away," Longarm frowned. "But if your Uncle Frank told your aunt to run and hide with you, how come she didn't?"

"All I can think of is that she made up her mind to stay with Uncle Frank and help him fight the Indians. I was at the edge of the sagebrush before I looked around and saw she wasn't with me. By then it was too late."

"Well, I can understand that easy enough," Longarm nodded. "There wasn't much sense in trying to help your kinfolks by the time you seen your aunt hadn't run with you."

Sarah shook her head. "I wasn't thinking whether or not it was sensible. By the time I looked back there was a solid line of Indians between me and them. You know, Marshal, I'm just beginning to realize now how lucky I was. I think the Indians were so interested in surrounding the wagon that they never even looked in my direction."

"So you just hunkered down and hid?"

"Well, not exactly. I didn't stop running for a long time even after I got in the sage. It took me a while to realize I was safe, and I guess I spent the better part of an hour trying to find my way back."

"By then, I reckon it was too late to do anything much."

"All I could do was watch, Marshal Long. I was so scared and so mad at myself for being scared that I guess I just didn't think of anything else. The Indians kept riding in a circle around the wagon, and all the time they kept on yelling and shooting."

"So they never noticed you, I guess?"

"Well, after I saw them, I stayed low. I kneeled down so the sage would hide me. Maybe if I'd had a gun I could've helped Uncle Frank and Glory, but the only two guns we had were in the wagon."

"That might've helped save your life, too," Longarm commented. "You'd have shot back, but I got a hunch them redskins might've been better shots."

"I never was very good with guns," Sarah confessed. "They always scared me a little bit, even after Lonnie—that's my older brother who got killed in the War—he tried to teach me how to use a gun, but I guess I didn't learn very much."

"It takes a while to learn shooting," Longarm said. He realized that Sarah needed to get her story told, to help flush the unhappy memory out of her mind, so he said nothing more.

After a moment, Sarah went on. "Uncle Frank and Glory shot back for a little while, then three or four of the Indians pulled out of the line and the next thing I knew they rode back waving torches and threw them at the wagon. Two of them landed on the canvas top and set fire to it. Then it was blazing up, and after a while Uncle Frank and Glory didn't shoot any more, and I realized they must be dead."

"But the Indians didn't leave right away, did they?"

Sarah shook her head. "No. I don't know when they left, though. After I understood that Uncle Frank and Glory must be dead, I laid down and started crying. I guess I cried myself to sleep, because when I woke up it was pitch dark and I cried some more and went to sleep again. Then—well, I woke up

14

when it was daylight, but I couldn't make myself move, even if I was thirsty, because I was sort of afraid to go look in the wagon. Then it was dark again, and I slept some more, and then after a while you rode up. I guess that's all there is to tell you."

Though Longarm had heard stories before which varied only in small details from the one Sarah had told him so haltingly, he nodded sympathetically.

"What you saw is going to be a mean thing in your mind for a while," he told her. "It'll come back and spook you now and again, but after a while you'll forget it, a little bit at a time. After that it won't be so bad."

"But what am I going to do now?" she asked him. "Uncle Frank and Glory were the only relatives I had left in the world, Marshal Long. I don't have a home, and what clothes and things I had were all burned with the wagon. I haven't anyplace to go or anybody to turn to."

"Then it looks like you'll have to depend on yourself from here on out," Longarm replied quietly. "Don't worry, you'll learn how. For starters, there's a new railroad line going to be built down into this part of Nevada pretty soon. That's going to bring a lot of new folks to settle here, and they'll be needing places to stay and food at mealtimes and all like that. You'll find a job before you know it."

"But until I do, Marshal Long?" Sarah asked. "I don't know where you're going, but I can't tag along with you or expect you to look after me."

"Now, that ain't quite right," he told her. "I'm heading for a railroad surveyors' camp right now. I'll take you along with me, and then we'll just have to see what happens."

"Taking care of me certainly can't be part of your job," she frowned. "You won't get into trouble, will you?"

"Not a bit," Longarm replied. "And keeping folks outa trouble's just about as much part of my job as getting 'em out of trouble once it starts. Now, it ain't too late to make a few miles today, and the quicker you get away from this wagon, the better it's going to be for you."

"I certainly agree with that, Marshal Long," Sarah nodded.

"You don't have anything to pack," Longarm went on.

"And I ain't unpacked my saddlebags, so we might as well get started. I know you're bound to be hungry, but I got some jerky in my saddlebags, and we can chew on it while we're moving."

Even at the slow pace to which Longarm kept the livery horse, talking was difficult. Though he had suggested that Sarah ride in the saddle, she'd refused. Pointing out that she'd done very little riding on horseback, she had insisted that Longarm stay in the saddle while she perched on the animal's rump.

Since Longarm had no idea how far they were from the surveying camp, he hadn't demurred too strenuously. The only alternative would have been for Sarah to share the saddle with him, which on a long ride would have been uncomfortable for both of them, so he'd opened his bedroll and taken out the blanket to spread across the animal's rump.

Slanting back to the trail he had left to investigate the buzzards, Longarm turned the livery horse west and kept it at a moderate gait as they began their journey in the late afternoon. They spoke little. For the first few miles after starting, both of them chewed on the jerky that Longarm produced from his saddlebags, and no food matches beef jerky for discouraging its eaters to indulge in idle chatter while they chew it.

Even after they had finished eating, Sarah and Longarm rode on in silence for quite a while before she broke the silence by asking, "I guess you must work out of Carson City, Marshal Long. Not that it's any of my business, but I've been wondering how you happened to be passing by the wagon."

"Nevada ain't my station, Miz Roundtree," Longarm replied. "I work outa the Denver office."

"Goodness! Isn't this a long way for you to be sent on a case?"

"Oh, it ain't such a much. A federal marshal's got the same authority anyplace he might be. It just depends on where his chief sends him."

"I see. Now, forgive me if I'm wrong, but from what you've said, you aren't real sure of exactly where you're being sent."

16

"If you put it that way, I ain't, Miz Roundtree. These surveyors I'm looking for is staking out the line for the railroad tracks, so I figure I might have to do a little zigging and zagging, but sooner or later I'll run into 'em."

"Well, that makes sense," Sarah said. After a moment of silence, she went on, "Could I ask you to do me a favor Marshal Long?"

"Why, sure."

"Would you mind just calling me Sarah instead of Mrs. Roundtree? I've been with my family so much since my husband died that I'm not used to being called anything else."

"I'll be real glad to. And I got a sorta nickname that my friends call me instead of Marshal Long. If I call you Sarah, you might as well call me Longarm. Like you say, it's friendlier, and besides, I answer to it better."

"Of course," she replied. Then, with the first happy chuckle Longarm heard her utter, she went on, "I see where your nickname must've come from. The long arm of the law, is that right?"

"That's how it got started," he agreed. "And I guess it'll be the same as long as I'm holding the job I got."

Exhaustion after her experiences of the past few days had soon overtaken Sarah, and she nodded drowsily as they made slow but steady progress along the single trail that cut across the level prairie. As the horse plodded steadily ahead, Longarm kept his mind busy going over the scanty information Billy Vail had given him before he'd left Denver.

"It's as much a mystery to me as it is to you why the big boss back in Washington insisted on having you put on this case," Vail had told Longarm after breaking the news of the new assignment that would take him to Nevada.

"Well, since you figure my orders must be coming right from the top, it's a pretty sure bet *somebody's* pulled some strings. It don't take more'n a teaspoon full of brains to figure that out," Longarm had replied. "I ain't had a case in Nevada for quite some time, but somebody out there likely remembered me."

"You must've really impressed whoever is asking for you,"

Vail said. "But, however it happened, they carry enough weight to go directly to the Justice Department in Washington instead of passing the request through the usual channels."

"It don't even sound to me like it's much of a case, Billy," Longarm had replied. "Sure, I know the Apache Kid, but I don't guess I know him any better'n I do them muckety-mucks back East. But, at that, I guess maybe I know him better'n any of the deputies out in Nevada do."

"Maybe that's why they asked for you instead of depending on the marshal's office in Carson City," Vail suggested.

"Seeing as my orders come from Washington, maybe I better not stir things up by reporting in at the chief marshal's office in Carson City and asking if they got anything that'll help me, then." Longarm frowned.

"It's your case," Vail replied. "Suit yourself about where you go and how you handle it. Not that you wouldn't anyhow. But if you don't want to start from Carson City, you don't have to. As far as I'm concerned, all you've got to do is show up out there ready to handle the job."

"I ain't had much time to think about it yet, Billy, but if that new railroad line's going to run north and south through the middle of Nevada there ain't much reason for me to go to Carson City at all. I don't reckon you got any idea where the rails are being laid?"

Vail had shaken his head, frowning thoughtfully, before he replied. "I'm not even sure they're ready to lay rails yet."

"Well, they're sure to have the line laid out."

"As I understand it, that line's going right through the middle of Nevada, which means it's going into that little pointed area at the southern tip of the state. And from what I've heard, that's where all the Apaches that aren't down on the Arizona border fighting General Miles or holed up in Mexico are squeezed up."

"They damn sure can't build a railroad without the line being surveyed," Longarm had pointed out. "And the way Nevada sorta squeezes up down in the south part, I'll be willing to take my chances about cutting across the right-of-way if I ride west from the SP."

"You'd probably save some time going that way, too," Vail

had replied with a thoughtful frown. "All I know is that the new line's supposed to run north and south, so if you'd rather not go to the Carson City office, you can take the Southern Pacific instead of the Union Pacific and try to find the survey party yourself."

"Now, that ought not to be such a much of a job," Longarm had replied. "So that's just what I'll aim to do."

"Like I said," Vail shrugged, "suit yourself. Just be sure you send me reports this time. You know what I get up against when we're handling a case that some local political bigwig is mixed up in."

"That's the part of this case that sticks in my craw, Billy," Longarm had replied. "Sometimes it looks like to me that we just got too many bosses."

"But it's still part of the job," Vail had pointed out. "When one of the men in the Washington office says jump, you and I hop, just like anybody else in the department does. But that's enough chatter. We'd better be talking business. Let's see, you brought in the Apache Kid before on some kind of a post-office robbery, if I remember correctly."

"You're close, but not close enough to get the cigar," Longarm said. "It was a mail-coach holdup way out in the Mormon country. But that don't mean it's gonna make it easier for me to run him down when he's on his own stomping grounds."

"Well, it might not be an easy case," Vail replied. "But this is one you can't blame on me. I'd a lot sooner put you on a case that'd keep you closer to home than send you so far away I can't keep tabs on you. But since I've got Washington riding on my back on this case, I want you to send me reports just as often as you can."

"Now, you didn't have no call to say that, Billy," Longarm protested. "Far as I recollect, I ain't let you down yet."

"You've delivered the goods when the chips were down," Vail admitted. "And I'm looking for you to do it again."

Breaking off, the chief marshal opened his desk drawer and took out a thin sheaf of papers.

Handing them to Longarm, he went on, "I made a few notes after I went through the file on the Apache Kid. Maybe they'll help you. At least they'll tell you where to start. One thing I'd forgotten and maybe you never did know about is that the Apache Kid didn't get a straight-out pardon. He was paroled, so he'll just go straight back to the pen when you bring him in."

"That'll at least save me having to sit through another trial," Longarm said as he stuffed the papers into his pocket.

Vail went on, "I told the clerk to make up your travel orders and vouchers, so you can pick them up at his desk when you go through the outside office. And remember, I need to know where you are and what you're doing."

"Unless it's changed more'n I figure, Nevada's mighty lonesome country, Billy," Longarm had reminded Vail as he took the papers and tucked them into his pocket. "But I'll do what I can."

Now, squinting into the declining sun, he began wondering how much farther he and Sarah would have to ride before they cut across the stakes placed by the railroad survey party he'd been told to look for.

Ahead, the desert-like terrain seemed as endless as it had been when he'd started out. There was nothing to break the long monotonous sweep of the gray-green sagebrush. Heat haze shimmering above the sun-baked land hid the horizon line. The haze divided the expanse ahead into three different strata, the soft greenish hue of the sage, above it the shimmering haze, and above the haze the sunset sky. The sun had disappeared by now below the haze, but an area which showed more brightness than usual marked its position. To the east, the approaching night was already beginning to deepen the sky's blue hue.

As Longarm twisted in the saddle to face the direction in which the horse was moving with plodding, tiring steps, Sarah stirred. "Goodness! I dozed off," she said. "I'm afraid I haven't been very good company for you, Longarm."

"Well, I can understand why you'd be tired, Sarah," Longarm replied. "You been through a lot the past few days. But we ain't going to be able to keep moving very much longer. I aim to pull up, the first place that looks good, and we'll stop there for the night."

"I don't mind admitting I'm tired," she replied. "And I'm getting hungry again. I'm as ready as you are to stop for the night."

Chapter 3

At some time during the night Longarm woke suddenly and sat up in his improvised bed. As always, he moved from sleep to wakefulness with his senses fully alert the instant his eyes opened. Before he could begin to figure out what had aroused him from a sound sleep, he got the answer. Somewhere nearby, the shrill neighing of one of the wild horses that roamed freely over Nevada's vast semi-deserts broke the night air. There was no way for Longarm to figure how far away the horse was, though the neigh had sounded very close indeed.

Being desert-wise, Longarm knew that even a small noise such as that made by a rabbit scurrying over the hard soil sounds loud and close in the quiet nights of that barren land. Settling back again, he tried to find a soft spot for his head on the pillow that he'd improvised from his shirt and saddlebags after giving Sarah his coat to fold into a pillow for herself. He closed his eyes, but before he'd gotten settled comfortably, Sarah spoke to him.

"Did that wild horse neighing wake you up too?"

"I guess it must've. A noise like that out here on the desert's enough to rouse anybody up."

"Do you suppose it wasn't a wild horse? Could it have been an Indian pony coming this way?" she asked.

"Not likely. It was a wild horse, all right. From the way it sounded, I'd guess it was looking for company. There's lots of them wild cayuses roaming around out here."

"How can you be sure?"

"Well, if you put it that way, Sarah, I don't guess I can be. But nobody who's got any sense goes traipsing across this desert country in the dark. Even the Indians don't generally move around much at night. Unless there's a full moon that gives a man or a horse light enough to see by, a critter can cripple itself by stepping into a crack in this hard dirt, or fall off a bluff. It don't take too much of a fall to kill either a horse or a man."

"Indians who know the country would ride around cliffs and crevasses, though."

"Likely they would. But they don't ramble in the dark any more'n a white man that knows the desert country does."

"Just the same, it upsets me to think about Indians being on the loose," she replied. After a few moments of silence she asked, "Longarm? Have you gone back to sleep already?"

"Not yet. Why?"

"Because I can't seem to get drowsy. I guess maybe I'm too nerved up," Sarah said. She lay quietly for a moment before asking, "Longarm, would you mind if I cuddled up to you? I think I'd sleep better if I could touch somebody, just to be sure I'm not all by myself again."

"Come ahead, if it'll make you feel better," Longarm agreed.

He was lying on his side on the shakedown pallet he'd improvised for them, using the horse blanket and the double blanket that formed his own bedroll. With the horse blanket unfolded and spread on the ground there was just enough room for them to lie side by side with their improvised pillows touching and Longarm's regular sleeping blanket covering both of them. Longarm lay quietly, after turning on his side, while Sarah pulled around to spoon herself against him, pressing his back. After a few moments he felt the warmth of her body through his longjohns.

Longarm did not move. Neither did Sarah, until several more minutes had slipped by. Then Sarah stirred and he felt her arm come to rest across his body. She lay motionless for a short while. Then, almost as though her arm was moving of its own accord, her hand slid slowly down Longarm's torso until it was resting on his hip. Longarm still lay quietly, though now he was thoroughly aware of the warmth of her soft, full breasts pressing against his back.

Sarah, too, stayed motionless for a few moments before her hand moved again. As though of its own volition, her hand crept slowly down Longarm's side. Her palm was open, and as her fingers slid over Longarm's hip they dipped down to his groin. After resting limply there for a few moments, they began exploring the bulge that was growing beneath his underwear. Involuntarily, Longarm stirred slightly as he began stiffening in response to Sarah's tentative caresses.

"You don't mind, do you?" she asked when he moved.

"I don't mind a bit, long as you're sure about what you're doing," he replied.

"Don't worry. I know quite well what I'm doing and I'm sure I want to do it. I've been wanting to ever since I saw you naked back there at the wagon."

"That wasn't your fault, or mine either," Longarm reminded her. "It was an accident."

"Accident or not, I saw you," Sarah went on. "And giving way to how I feel might not be the right thing for me to do, after everything that's happened. I've told myself a dozen times since we've been lying here to stop thinking about having you in me, and right now I'm telling myself to stop feeling you and thinking about you, but it's not doing any good at all. And feeling you swell up in my hand this way, I'm glad it isn't."

Sarah increased the pressure of her hand, and Longarm knew that the time had come for him to make the decision his sensations had been urging on him for several minutes. He

25

turned to lie facing her. To his surprise, Sarah was naked. No fabric intruded between his hands and her softly bulging breasts.

Longarm caressed the warm soft globes with his fingertips and tongue, feeling their tips protrude erect as he continued his attentions. Sarah's warm hands moving more and more urgently on him and the warmth and softness of her breasts under his own hands combined irresistably to urge him on.

Sarah sensed his decision, and hers had already been made. She threw one leg over his hips and pulled herself closer to him, then placed the tip of his rigid shaft in the moist warmth that was awaiting it. Longarm drove into her with a long fast lunge that brought a gasp of pleased surprise from her throat. She rolled onto her back and locked her thighs around Longarm's hips to pull him even more deeply into her.

"Oh, how wonderful!" she sighed. "It's been such a long time since I've been with a man that I'd almost forgotten what it's like!"

Longarm did not reply, but sought her lips with his. She offered them eagerly, and for a few moments they lay motionless, content with the pleasure of their joining. Then Sarah stirred and Longarm took her move for an invitation. He began thrusting with a steady measured rhythm.

Beginning to moan now, Sarah started to meet his measured lunges, but her slow movements lasted for only a few minutes. Suddenly she cried out and began quivering. Longarm speeded his thrusting and within a few seconds Sarah began rolling her hips, thrashing frantically as she moved, her legs gripping Longarm's hips in a tightening embrace until she cried out in delight.

After a few moments she sighed and said, "I've been without a man in my life too long. I'd almost forgotten the feelings you just gave me, Longarm."

"I'm glad you're pleased," he told her. "It goes against nature for a woman to do without a man after she's got used to having one in bed with her. Though I got to admit, this ain't much of a bed."

"It's better than no bed at all," Sarah reminded him. "And while I was hiding from the Indians out in the sagebrush last night, I'd have been real glad to've had even a makeshift."

"We better be thinking about going back to sleep," he told her. "Else we'll be too tired to start moving on when daylight gets here."

"Moving on is the last thing I'm thinking about," Sarah replied. "I'd just as soon stay right here."

"If you put it that way, so would I, Sarah. But I got my case to think about, and the faster we move the sooner I'm going to get started on it."

"I suppose you've got a wife waiting for you back in Denver, too."

"You're supposing wrong. A man that holds down the kind of job I do ain't got any business marrying, not unless he finds a woman that don't mind carrying around the idea she might get to be a widow real sudden."

"That hadn't occurred to me," Sarah said soberly. "But I can understand—" A yawn she could not suppress interrupted her and when she'd stopped gaping she abandoned the thought she had started to explore and said, "I guess you're right. All of a sudden I'm ready to go to sleep. Good night again, Longarm."

Without waiting for him to reply, Sarah pulled her blanket over her shoulders and closed her eyes. In a moment she was breathing deeply. Longarm watched her for a moment, then followed her example and was soon asleep himself.

"Longarm, we'd surely have come across some sign of those surveyors, if they'd come down into this part of the state." Sarah frowned as Longarm reined in at the rim of the long slope that stretched ahead. He stood up in his stirrups to get a better look as he gazed across the vast expanse of sagebrush that stretched in front of them.

"I ain't so sure about that," Longarm replied. He glanced at the sun, almost directly overhead, and went on, "But we've covered a pretty good stretch without resting the horse, so we better get our feet on the ground and let the nag rest a while."

He swung out of the saddle and helped Sarah down. They stood on the top of the upslope they had just reached. Longarm gazed at it through the smoke of a freshly lighted cheroot that writhed around his head in the windless air of the prairie.

"We could pass close to where the surveyors are working and never even see 'em," he told her. "Not that I think we have, but it could happen that way. Chances are, though, they're up ahead of us someplace. That'd all depend on the lay of the land up to the north of here."

"I don't understand," she said.

"Well, there's a great big belt of mountains that cuts right across Nevada to the north of here. The surveyors have got to pick out grades for the track that a locomotive hauling a string of ore cars can top, which means the line's going to meander around some from east to west."

"You know, I've often wondered why railroads wind around so much in hilly country, but now I understand," Sarah told him. "Then after they get into this flat country we're crossing right now, the rails will go in a straight line, I guess."

"Just as straight as a tight string," Longarm nodded. "And as far as I can tell from the map I'm carrying, this long level stretch we're crossing now is called Frenchman Flat."

"Well, it's certainly flat," Sarah smiled. "But I'd like to know where the Frenchman comes in."

"Now, that's something I can't say." Longarm told her. "I guess there must've been a Frenchman along with whoever crossed this part of the country first. Was it left up to me I'd call it Digger Flat or, if I wanted to be polite to the redskins, it'd be Paiute Flat."

"Those are Indian tribes, I guess?"

"Not different tribes. One tribe with some offshoots."

"Just one tribe that has two names?" Sarah asked, raising her eyebrows.

"Three names, if you come right down to brass tacks," Longarm answered. "Ho's short for Hohokam, and that's the same as the Paiutes, and they're the Diggers, too, the way some of 'em explained it to me. Only some of them professors that works for the Indian Bureau got 'em mixed up with the other Utes. Leastwise, that's what the redskins say."

"Why don't the professors listen to what the Indians themselves say?"

"Shucks, Sarah, professors can't listen for talking. They already got their minds made up. Indians, now, they set pretty straight lines for what they're after. I guess you found out when they jumped your kinfolks' wagon, they'd sometimes sooner shoot us than talk to us."

Sarah shook her head. "I guess it's too confusing for me to understand."

"If you think it's mixed up out here, you better stay away from the Indian Nation, then," Longarm told her. "There's tribes from the East back there, like the Cherokees and Crees, that ain't a bit like the wild bands we still got roaming around in this part of the country."

"It sounds to me like you know a lot about Indians," Sarah remarked. "Do you men on the marshal's force have a lot of trouble with them?"

"We do now and again, but we try not to get mixed up with 'em unless they get into one of our cases. The Indian Bureau's supposed to look after them." Longarm squinted at the sun and went on, "We been resting quite a while, Sarah. If you're freshened up enough, let's get moving again. There ain't no telling how much farther we'll be riding before we run into that surveying outfit."

Longarm clasped his hands and bent down to let Sarah put one foot in them. Before he could boost her up to the horse's rump, a rifle cracked in the distance and the slug whistled through the air where his head would have been if he hadn't bent forward. He pulled his hands apart while the whine of the slug still vibrated between them and grabbed Sarah's arm with one hand while he was reaching for the horse's reins with the other.

His movements were so swift that Sarah had no time to ask questions or to protest before Longarm was dragging her and the horse down the little slope ahead. An expression of bewilderment was still on her face when he pulled her to the ground with him. Another shot broke the desert silence and whistled dangerously close to the livery horse. Sarah raised her head when she heard the report.

Longarm pushed her head down and said sternly, "Don't try to look up or get up!"

As he spoke he was scrambling to his feet himself. He stepped to the horse's head and by wrestling the animal's bit to twist its neck forced the horse to fall flat on its side. He went to his knees when the horse fell, then flattened himself on the ground between Sarah and the horse, still holding firmly to the upcurved ends of the animal's bit.

"Chances are it's one of the redskins that killed your folks who's doing that shooting," he told her. "Likely he went back to the wagon to try to pick up some loot and while he was noseying around he seen our tracks. Then he followed 'em till he caught up with us here."

"But why do the Indians want to kill us?" she asked. "We haven't done them any harm!"

"I ain't got time to explain that now," Longarm told her. "Just take my word that I know what I'm talking about and do like I tell you to."

Belly-crawling around the horse, Longarm slipped his rifle from its saddle scabbard and levered a shell into the chamber. He gazed around the area looking for a vantage point. The best he could find was a low rise on the edge of the slope. Jumping to his feet, then bending low, he ran to the little rise.

Fully aware that he was inviting the sniper's fire, but trusting the finely honed reactions that had saved him from death many times before, Longarm rose to his full height and quickly scanned the barren landscape. He spotted the Indian pony almost at once, a quarter of a mile back in the stretch of ground that he and Sarah had so recently crossed, but he could see no sign of the sniper.

Suddenly the Indian popped up from the brush between Longarm and the horse. Longarm got a fleeting glimpse of the man's face before the Indian dropped his head to meet the stock of the rifle he was raising. In readiness for sudden action, Longarm had already shouldered his Winchester, and his finger was on the trigger. Before the sniper could bring his weapon up to aim, Longarm snapshotted.

He heard the solid thwack of lead on wood as his slug tore into the stock of the Indian's rifle, sending the man tumbling backward. Pumping fast, Longarm bracketed the spot where his adversary had fallen. Although he had little faith in blind

30

shooting, Longarm got off four shots in quick succession, shifting his point of aim each time he fired.

Suddenly the Indian burst from the thigh-high sage and dived for his horse. Longarm swung the Winchester, his trigger finger tightening as the rifle moved. The Indian was leaping for his pony when Longarm's finger tightened on the trigger. He knew instantly that he had miscounted his shots when the hammer clicked on an empty chamber.

By now the fleeing redskin had mounted and was galloping away. Longarm knew the distance was far too great for his Colt to be effective, and he did not even go through the futile motion of drawing the pistol. All that he could do was stand and watch the fleeing sniper put still more distance between them. Frustrated and angry with himself for having failed to keep track of the shells he'd spent, Longarm turned away and started back to the spot where he'd left Sarah and the horse.

She asked the question with her eyes, her brows rising inquiringly. Longarm shook his head and said, "I played the fool and let him get away. But I got a good look at him, and I know who he is."

"You've seen him before?" Sarah asked.

"I've put handcuffs on him," Longarm replied. "And it's my job right now to put 'em on him again, because he was paroled outa the pen after he promised he'd go straight. Unless I made an awful bad mistake, he's a fellow that calls himself the Apache Kid. I hauled him in the first time, that was going on three years ago, for a bank holdup over in Mormon country."

"I hope you're not planning to leave me here while you chase him," Sarah said.

"I ain't that kind of fool, Sarah. He'd be in a hidey-hole someplace a long time before I could track him down. Besides, I got a job to do here, and that comes first. No, we'll go see if we can find that surveying party I'm supposed to locate. The Apache Kid will just have to wait a while, till I've got time to go after him. Now let's mount up and be on our way."

Chapter 4

"I sorta figured we'd get lucky if we just kept pushing on to the west like we been doing," Longarm told Sarah as he pointed ahead.

Sarah looked at the peeled tree branch, glowing with the bright yellow of fresh wood, that rose above the low-growing sage a mile or so ahead. The slender stake had a flutter of red cloth strips hanging from its top. The strips were barely stirring in the light pre-sunset breeze.

"Does that pole mean we've found the surveying party?" she asked.

"Well, we ain't exactly found 'em yet, but we've come to the line they're setting," Longarm explained. "We know they're moving southwards, so all we got to do now is go on to that stake and look around till we see the next one, then we go on to it, and spot the ones they've set later on. Pretty soon we'll catch up with 'em."

"How much farther do you think we'll have to go before we find them?"

"That's hard to tell, Sarah. Wait till we get to that stake up ahead. For all I can tell this far away, it could've been set a month or so ago, or it mighta been set yesterday. I'll know more as soon as I take a close look at it."

They rode on to the stake. Longarm swung out of the saddle and helped Sarah down. Then they walked over to the stake. He peered closely at the strip of red cloth that was tacked on to the top of the wooden slat, then examined the few wagon-wheel ruts that broke the sagebrush a few yards beyond the stake.

"We ain't too far behind 'em." he announced. "The cloth on that stake ain't a bit dirty or worn, and the wood's just as bright as the day it was peeled. And these wagon tracks is fresh. Look how they cut over the old ones. I don't imagine it's been more'n two or three days since they passed by here."

"Then we ought to catch up with them in another day or so," Sarah said. "Unless that Indian comes back and brings some more along with him."

"Which he's likely to do," Longarm nodded. "Now let's see if we can spot the next stake and start for it without wasting any more time."

He scanned the flat, featureless landscape and in a matter of a few seconds saw the stake he was seeking, a small strip of color against the pale green sage.

"There we are, Sarah," he said. "If all the rest are as easy to find as it was, we ain't got a thing in the world to worry about now."

"Except the Indians," she suggested. "If we can see these stakes, they can too."

"We'll worry about that if the redskins take after us," Longarm replied matter-of-factly. "Except for that one that I swapped shots with, they ain't showed no signs yet they're going to give us any more trouble."

"Let's get started," Sarah suggested. Then she added, "It's funny, Longarm. While we were looking for this stake, I didn't really think we had a chance of finding it. Now that we have, I'm anxious to see where they'll lead us."

"Well, one thing's for sure," Longarm told her. "I'll be as glad as you when we catch up. We'll just about be outa jerky by tomorrow night, and there sure ain't no stores closer'n a four- or five-day ride where we can buy more grub. And by this time tomorrow, we'll be needing more water, even if we have been real careful about taking just a swallow or two."

"I was afraid you were going to say you'd be glad to see somebody besides me," Sarah smiled.

"Now, you know that ain't a fact, Sarah!" he protested.

"I hope not. Anyhow, I was just making a joke."

"Joking's fine, and it don't bother me a bit," Longarm told her soberly. "But riding trail with an empty belly ain't nothing to joke about. And there's something else I got on my mind that's a heap more important. If them Indians do take a notion to come after us, we're going to need more than just one rifle and a pistol to hold 'em off, or we're likely to wind up without no hair."

Mounting the livery horse again, they headed for the next survey stake. When they reached it they spotted the one beyond it. They kept moving from one stake to the next until darkness overtook them. They made a dry camp that night, and the few bites of jerky washed down with a scanty sip of water did nothing to lessen the pleasure of their lovemaking, nor did the occasional scurrying noises of small animals in the sagebrush disturb their sleep.

"It looks like we're finally getting close to them surveyors," Longarm said, squinting under his hatbrim at the descending sun. "And just about time, too. If we don't catch up to that bunch before dark, we won't have no supper to speak of."

"You said a little while ago that they couldn't be very far ahead now," Sarah reminded him. "Have you found something that's made you change your mind?"

"No, not exactly. Except the wheel marks and the hoofprints don't seem no fresher than they was when we picked 'em up. But all we can do is keep on moving. Maybe if we don't run into 'em before dark, we'll get to wherever they are before we get too hungry tomorrow."

After the long grind it had endured during Longarm's ride from the spot in Mormon territory where he'd gotten off the Southern Pacific train, and the double load it had carried for two days, the livery horse was showing signs of tiring. In spite of his urge to push the animal, Longarm kept a very light hand on the reins and made frequent short stops to rest the animal.

As the long day wore to its close, he began looking for a place to stop. Except for the stakes marking the future railroad grade, they still hadn't seen any trail signs to indicate that they were closer to the surveyors. Longarm had almost decided to rein in when he squinted ahead and saw a thin, almost invisible wisp of smoke rising against the darkening sky. He pointed it out to Sarah.

"Looks like we're getting there at last," he said. "If that ain't them surveyors up ahead, I'll eat my Stetson, even if we ain't got enough water to wash it down with."

"I certainly hope so," Sarah told him. "I'm getting thirstier by the minute."

After another long half-hour of ever-slower progress, with the sun gone and the sky darkening steadily, they could see the faint flicker of a campfire. The fire seemed to grow brighter as the dusk deepened. It was an easy beacon to follow for the last two miles to the spot where a small group of men sat hunkered down around a tiny campfire. By the light of the flames, Longarm and Sarah could see not only the men, but three wagons with their white canvas tops a short distance from the fire, and the rope corral that penned the party's animals.

As they drew closer and the vague shadows silhouetted by the small tongue of flame took shape and form, they counted five men around the fire. In another few moments, when the men heard the thudding of the livery horse's hooves and stood up to peer into the gathering gloom, the members of the party could be separated into individuals rather than dark shapes.

One was a black man, his face shining in the reflected firelight. Two of them wore straggly beards, untrimmed and tangled; the other two whites and the black man were clean-shaven. All five wore sturdy denim trousers and knee-high lace-up boots, both boots and clothing stained and showing signs of wear. Each of them had on a pistol belt, and two had picked up rifles as they stood up. Their features were not easy

36

to distinguish, for they stood with their backs to the fire watching Longarm and Sarah approach, the blaze throwing their faces into shadow.

Longarm began speaking even before he had reined in. "I sure hope you fellows are the ones we're looking for," he said. "If you're the ones that're surveying for a new railroad, we've finally caught up with you."

"Damned if it don't seem like you know a lot about our business, stranger," one of the men said, stepping forward. "No offense meant, but maybe you better tell us who you are."

Before Longarm could reply, one of the men poked the man standing beside him and said without lowering his voice, "Hey, look-a there! Them ain't two men! One of 'em's a woman!"

"So she is," Longarm said quickly, then turned to the man who had spoken first. "My name's Long. I'm a deputy United States marshal outa the Denver office. The lady's name is Sarah Roundtree, and she's traveling with me because a two-day ride back from here the wagon her and her folks was traveling in got jumped by a bunch of redskins."

"I guess you got a badge or papers of some kind to back up who you say you are?" asked the man.

"Sure." Longarm produced his wallet and opened it to flash his badge in the reflecting firelight. "Now, the reason I been looking for you is because there's an Indian man someplace close around here that goes by the name of the Apache Kid, and I've come to take him in."

"If he's the one that's behind all the trouble we been having with the damned Indians, you can take him and welcome," one of the surveyors said.

"That goes for me, too," another one seconded. "Ever since we started across these flats, we haven't had anything but trouble with 'em."

"All right, men, let's hold up on the talk," said the one who had been the first to speak to Longarm. "Let's wait and do our talking later." Turning back to Longarm, he went on, "From the way you folks look, dusty and riding double and all that, I've got an idea you'd like to have a rest and likely something to eat before we do anything else."

"Water, first!" Sarah broke in, her voice raspy. "Longarm didn't have but the one canteen-full, and we've been on short rations for the last day or so."

"Well, two of the wagons over yonder've got water barrels on them, and we top 'em off at every spring or creek we come to where the water's not too alkalied," the man who seemed to be the party's boss said. "I guess you're thirstier than you are hungry, so you two go have a fill-up and I'll see what we can stir up in the way of grub."

While the surveyor was talking, Longarm had dismounted and helped Sarah to the ground. She started at once to the wagons, carrying Longarm's canteen, while Longarm walked up to the fire with the surveyor who had taken charge of things.

"From the way you was talking, I made a guess you're the boss of this bunch," Longarm said.

"As far as anybody else is, I guess," the man replied. "My name's Jared Foster, and most folks finds Jared a hard name to handle, so I just go by Jay."

"Well, I got sorta the same trouble," Longarm nodded. "My friends began calling me Longarm a while back, so I answer to it now a lot faster'n I do my right name."

Foster nodded, and the two shook hands. Then, pointing as he talked, Foster began pointing to the others. "That's Clem Hobbs, and the one next to him's Sandy Brown. Now, I know that black fellow's got a first name because I've seen it on the pay slips, but he answers best if you just call him Cross. And next to him is Red O'Grady."

Longarm had acknowledged each of the introductions with a nod or gesture. As the men began stirring to put together a meal for him and Sarah, he turned to Foster again.

"These Indians you was talking about," he frowned. "They'd be Apaches, I guess?"

"I wouldn't know about that, Marshal." Foster replied. "I just know they've made a lot of trouble for us, and some of it's been big trouble. They killed Mose Barton three days ago. Just came swooping out of a cut in a little mesa, yelling and shooting, when Mose and Cross started past, and if Cross hadn't been a good shot I'd be shy two men now instead of just one."

"I didn't see any sign of a grave while we were following your stakes here," Longarm frowned.

"I guess we did a good job of hiding the grave, then," the black man said as he came up carrying two plates heaped with bully-beef and boiled potatoes. "I've heard some Indians will dig up a grave to get the scalp off of a man they've killed, so we moved a few of them sagebrush plants and put 'em on top of where we buried him and tried to hide the signs that showed where we'd been digging."

While Cross was talking, Sarah had rejoined the group. She handed Longarm the canteen she had filled and he sipped from it, holding the water in his mouth a moment before swallowing. He picked up the conversation quickly when Cross paused.

"My guess is it was that same bunch of redskins that jumped the wagon Sarah was traveling on with her kinfolks," he said. "They'd set fire to it and one of 'em was still lurking around. He's taken a few shots at us while we was on the way here."

"His aim must not've been very good," Foster suggested.

Longarm shook his head as he replied, "It wasn't, and mine didn't turn out to be much better. He scatted fast when I begun shooting back."

"A pity you didn't get him," Foster said. "But we can talk about the redskins later. You and the lady're bound to be real hungry by now. Just hunker down and be comfortable while you eat, and then we can talk some more."

Neither Longarm nor Sarah need a second suggestion. The men around the fire made room for them and passed only a few casual remarks among themselves while the two began eating. By the time they had finished and put their plates aside, the spirits of both had improved. As he lighted an after-supper cheroot, Longarm ran his eyes around the men circling the fire, and as soon as his cigar was drawing satisfactorily, turned back to Foster.

"You got quite a good-sized bunch in your outfit," he said.

"But I guess you got a pretty big job, too."

"Hell, any surveying job's a big one in country like this," Foster replied. "Broken-up, rough as a cob, and dry as a bone to boot. But the fact is we're a man short right now, since poor old Mose Barton got killed, and I don't know when or how we're going to get a man to take his place."

"I take it that your man was killed when them Indians jumped you after you'd started going across Frenchman Flat?" Longarm asked.

"Right as rain, they did," Foster nodded. "Just Mose's wagon, though. He was teamed up with Cross that day. I guess you know how we set our lines, don't you?"

"Well, I've seen it done, here and there," Longarm nodded. "But I don't know all that much about surveying."

"We roll two men to a wagon," Foster explained. "Two of the wagons go ahead of the last one, but they're just scouting; they don't try to set grade. But the way we work keeps the wagons apart, so it was easy for the Indians to pick Mose off."

"I guess I don't understand why you need three crews," Longarm said. "Splitting up like you do don't seem to me to make a lot of sense."

"Saves a lot of time," Foster went on. "Even if they all aren't actually full crews. Hobbs goes ahead in the big wagon just to scout out the general lay of the land and eyeball the grades. He puts down temporary stakes for the crew in the second wagon to work from. Sandy Brown is working by himself right now, but his job is to fine things up a little bit more and make sure there's no bad places the first wagon missed. O'Grady and Cross put the stakes down after they shoot the grades with a theodolite. Then finally I come along to check and make sure everything's right and we won't have to backtrack and do a stretch over again."

"What you're doing is figuring the best place that a train can get up without having to slow down too much, then?" Sarah asked Foster.

"That's about the size of it, ma'am," the surveyor agreed. "If it was just a horse and wagon road grade, we wouldn't go to all that trouble, but this is railroad grade we're shooting.

Even half a degree of rise in a mile makes one hell of a lot of difference to a loaded train trying to go up it."

"Curves have to be just right, too," one of the men by the fire volunteered.

"You can't move very fast, then," Longarm frowned.

"Nope," Foster replied. "In rough country we'll do maybe five or six miles a day. Over level ground where we don't run into dry washes or gullies, we might do ten."

"Well, you've just answered a question that's been in my mind that I hadn't got around to asking," Longarm went on. "You see, I got a half-hunch about them Indians, and I think I know the one that's stirring 'em up. I was hoping I'd find some place where Sarah's going to be safe, and it looks like your outfit will just suit things to a tee. What'd you say to her staying with your bunch a few days, while I head for the place where that Indian caught up with us and see if I can backtrack him."

"You didn't mention that idea to me before, Longarm," Sarah protested.

"I didn't take the notion to do it before we run into Foster and his crew," Longarm replied.

"Now, hold on, Marshal Long!" Foster said. "My men have got to keep moving. We've got a railroad survey to finish, and the man that's paying us won't like the idea of a woman tagging along and being underfoot!"

"Who says I'd be underfoot?" Sarah demanded.

"Why, I—" Foster began.

She cut him short, saying, "You just told us you're short a man. Why can't I take his place?"

"This gets to be a rough job sometimes," Foster told her. "It's a man's work."

"I've done enough of what folks call man's work to know what that means about half the time," she replied tartly. "And from what you've said and what I've seen, the hardest job you're doing is pounding a few branches in the ground and tying little strips of cloth on top of them. If you're worried about me being able to handle a horse and wagon, I've been doing that since I was ten years old. Now give me one good

41

reason why I can't replace that man you've lost, and do as good a job as he did."

When Foster did not reply at once, Longarm took up where Sarah left off. He said soberly, trying to hold back the smile that persisted in forming on his face, "I seen this lady come out off the prairie after she'd got away from the redskins that murdered her only relatives, and I been traveling with her for a couple of days now. You don't need to worry about her not pulling her weight if you take her on with your crew. She'll do that and a little bit more besides."

For a moment the surveyor was silent, then he said with a frown, "I'm going to have to think about it some, Longarm."

"Now, don't take me wrong," Longarm said, choosing his words carefully and keeping his voice levelly neutral. "But you know what I can do if I take a notion to, I guess?"

"I think you just moved out of my range," Foster frowned. "Maybe you'd better spell it out."

"Why, I could deputize you or any of your men or your whole crew, if it comes down to it. Then you'd be officers of the law and I'd be in charge of you as long as I needed your help."

"Now, hold on!" Foster protested. "We've already got one boss! Barton Calder's railroad company is hiring us!"

Hearing the name of the man who had progressed from being a kingpin gambler to one of Nevada's richest and most respected financiers gave an instant answer to a lot of the questions which had stayed in Longarm's mind after Billy Vail had given him his assignment.

"You mean Calder's the man putting up the money to build this railroad?" he asked.

"Sure," Foster nodded. "I thought everybody knew that. Of course, there's others in it with him, but don't make any mistake about it, he's the real boss."

"And he's a man who swings enough political weight in Washington to get me put on this case," Longarm said. "Even if my chief didn't call no names, Calder's the only one who could get the Justice Department to send me clear from Denver to settle things with them redskins that's been giving you trouble."

"Are you sure about that?" Foster asked.

"I'm sure," Longarm nodded. "And it makes things easier for both of us. You won't have a thing to worry about if you put Sarah on your crew, and that's something I'll guarantee you."

Chapter 5

Foster stared at Longarm for a moment, then asked, "How come you're so free in promising that a big man like Barton Calder will do something for you?"

"Because Bart Calder's a man that keeps his word," Longarm replied quietly. "And he told me whatever I needed that he could do or give, all I had to do was let him know."

"You sure must've done him one hell of a big favor," Foster said. However, the tone of his voice showed that Longarm's simple statement had been effective. He went on, "Well, if that's how it is, and if Miz Roundtree's agreeable—"

"Don't worry," Sarah broke in quickly. "I'm agreeable, and I'll do the best I can to hold up my end of the bargain. I ran away from the Apaches once, but that wasn't because I was afraid of them. I didn't have a gun, and I thought I was helping to save my aunt. But I'll never run again!"

"That oughta satisfy you," Longarm told the surveyor.

"Except for one thing," Foster answered. Turning to Cross, he asked, "You got any objections?"

"Not a one," the black man shrugged. "As long as Miz

Sarah can handle the wagon and a gun, I'll do the rest, like I always did when I was partnering with Mose."

"That reminds me of one more thing," Foster went on, turning to Sarah. "I hope you know how to handle a rifle."

"Rifle or pistol, I can usually hit what I'm aiming at," she answered levelly. "If the Apaches hadn't set fire to my kinfolks' wagon I'd have fought them to a finish. And where those outlaw Indians are concerned, I'm not likely to forget how they killed my kinfolks."

"I guess that oughta satisfy you, Foster," Longarm said.

"We've got a deal," the survey party leader nodded. "I'm taking your word that you'll back me up if the boss raises any kind of a fuss."

"Like I said, you don't have to worry about him," Longarm replied, getting to his feet. "Now, I don't know about the rest of you, but I'm about ready for my bedroll. I aim to start backtracking on them outlaw Apaches soon as it's light enough to see."

"I certainly hope you catch them!" Sarah said. She turned to Foster. "I guess I can borrow a blanket or two until we get to a town where I can buy some of my own."

"If you're not spooked by the idea, you can take Mose's bedroll," Foster replied.

"That won't bother me a bit," Sarah told him.

"And you can sleep in the wagon, if you've got a mind to," Cross put in. "Mose always did. I bunked on the ground when I was partnering with him after I found out he snored so loud that he'd wake me up a dozen times a night."

"Looks like everything's settled, then," Longarm said. "Except I'll need to draw on you for some grub, Foster."

"Sure. Come on over to my wagon with me and I'll fix you up now. Then you can start whenever you please tomorrow morning."

Longarm was fast asleep when Sarah's whisper woke him. He came to his senses instantly, fully alert.

"What's wrong?" he asked her.

"Nothing's wrong, Longarm. I just wanted to say thank you for helping me before you go, and I was afraid if I waited

46

until tomorrow you'd be gone before I got up."

"Why, you don't owe me no thanks, Sarah, even if it is real nice of you to think about me."

"Thinking about you is what brought me here, not just to thank you and say good-bye. And I won't lie to you. There's nothing I'd like better than to crawl into your bedroll with you," she went on. "That's the other reason I came over. But I got to wondering if it'd be wise."

Longarm sat up in his blankets and looked around. He'd gone a little way apart from the others, planning to start as soon as the dawnlight broke the night sky. The fire was no more than a bed of glowing coals by now, but in the moonless night even its red glow cast enough light over the wagons and blanketed forms of the sleeping men to enable him to see that none of them were stirring. A few muted snores reached his ears, further assurance that they were sleeping soundly.

"You decide what you feel like doing, Sarah," Longarm said. "You'll sure be welcome, but if you say no, I can see why."

Sarah hesitated no longer. She slid into the bedroll beside Longarm and he took her in his arms. After a few minutes, her sighs of pleasure and the muted whispers of noise as their bodies entwined were added to the snores of the surveying party.

Longarm had no trouble backtrailing the hoofprints of his livery horse, and the brassy glint of his spent cartridge case shining from the ground identified the spot where he had exchanged shots with the Indian who had tried to kill him and Sarah. Reining in, he spent several minutes studying the lay of the land in the area from which their attacker had fired, then he toed the horse toward the spot where he had glimpsed the retreating Indian.

As he'd expected, he saw signs of the sniper's presence at once. The most obvious was a scattering of wilting sagebrush strewn beside an area where there were a half-dozen of the scrubby brushes that had been pushed to earth and were still slantwise to the surrounding growth. The two separate messages they sent were both crystal-clear.

That's where he was laying, Longarm told himself as his slitted eyes traversed the spot. *Stretched out flat on his belly while he watched me and Sarah for a spell. There was some leaves twigging outa them bushes in front of him that kept him from getting a clear look, so he tweaked 'em away so's he could see without having to move his head around.*

Leading away from the place where the sage had been pressed down, Longarm noticed several spots where tender young shoots of the ground growth had been crushed and broken by running feet. Beyond the area where the growth had been bent he saw the gleam of freshly splintered wood, golden-brown against the light green sage.

Walking slowly to where the splinters lay scattered, Longarm recognized them as having been blasted by the slug of his Winchester from the stock of the Apache's rifle. A few of the long jagged bits of walnut showed dark stains, and Longarm bent over one of them to be sure the stains had been made by blood.

You didn't miss getting him by much, old son, he thought as he peered at the reddish-brown blotches against the light tan of the torn wood. *Might even say you did get him, in a way. And you'll sure know him right off when you catch up with him. Them splinters must've cut into his face pretty good.*

A few yards past the splinters the ground slanted downward sharply into the saucer-like hollow of a little vale where the sage grew sparsely on the barren soil. Horse droppings lay scattered in one spot and even had they not been there, Longarm would have known that the ambusher had tethered his pony in the hollow, where it would not be seen by anyone passing through the area. At several places on the spots of ground where there was no growth, the prints of an unshod horse had cut half-moons into the flaked soil. The prints led across the hollow and up on the opposite side.

"Well, it looks like that's all she wrote," Longarm said aloud as he took a cigar from his vest pocket and lighted it. "From here on out it oughta be real easy to track him, leastways as long as he kept his cayuse galloping. Which might not be all that far, seeing as how you couldn't take after him

48

right then. But the only way to find out is to start and see how far you can get before you run into him or run outa tracks."

Trailing a thin line of blue cigar smoke behind him, Longarm walked back to his horse. Swinging into the saddle, he toed the animal past the spot where the sniper had hidden and took up the trail of the Indian's pony where it led out of the hollow.

For the first few miles, following the trail left by the Indian pony was fairly easy. The sniper had ridden in as straight a line as possible, angling to the north, away from the vestigial east-west road Longarm had followed on his way to the area. In the country he'd entered now there were many places where the sage grew so densely that not even an ant could have passed through the growth without leaving some kind of trail. Even though the sage covered the land more completely here, occasionally he crossed a spot where alkali or mineral deposits close to the surface inhibited the growth of even the sturdy sagebrush. Across such areas, the broken arcs left by the hooves of his quarry's galloping mount showed clearly.

From the character of the hoofmarks it was clear to Longarm that the Indian had made no effort to hide the prints or to zigzag his pony through the areas where the sage grew thickest. He found that he could keep his livery horse to a fast but not overly tiring pace, reining it in only occasionally in areas where the sage grew thickest and its leaves hid the ground completely. In such spots he twitched the reins and pulled the horse down to a slower gait that gave him more time to examine the ground.

Longarm had ridden perhaps four or five miles before he saw what his years of riding the West had given him full confidence that he would find. Between him and the horizon, where the sage grew taller and its green was a shade or two darker than the growth through which he'd been traveling, a dozen or so rounded humps broke the level skyline. He headed the horse toward them.

After another half-hour the humps could now be seen as round-topped huts. A small patch of bright green covered the ground's surface for a short distance behind them, its more brilliant hue contrasting sharply with the lighter gray-green of the seemingly endless sea of sagebrush. As Longarm drew still closer he could see the dark forms of people working in the green patch behind the huts. The workers saw him almost as soon as he had seen them, and by the time he reached the village the green field behind it was deserted and a score of Indians had gathered into a huddle in front of the huts.

Longarm was close enough now to make out details. Even at a distance he had placed the crude beehive-shaped hovels as belonging to the poorest and least highly regarded of the Ho or Hohokam sub-tribes, the Diggers. The two dozen men and women who stood in a straggled bunch in front of the huts bore out his earlier assumption. The men wore only breech-clouts, the women had on short shapeless dresses made from ragged scraps of different kinds of cloth pieced together, and the few children were totally naked.

Distant relatives of the Pueblo tribes to the east, the Diggers did not welcome civilization or adopt its ways as did their more advanced cousins. They were a primitive and peaceful people, but though friendly to all, they remained a small, reclusive tribe which shunned contact not only with the whites, but with other Indian tribes as well. The Diggers made clear by their actions that they preferred to avoid trouble and asked nothing more than to be left alone. Separated as they were by choice from white settlers and other Indians alike, the Diggers were only now beginning to learn how to live a settled existence in villages and to plant and harvest crops. In earlier days they had moved with the seasons in small bands, living on the roots of whatever sparse edible vegetation was to be found in the arid, unfriendly desert land to which the Diggers had been driven by the warrior tribes, the Apaches and Navajos.

A few yards in front of the Indians, Longarm reined in and raised his right hand, palm outward. One of the three old men who stood near the center of the group replied by repeating the sign. He was obviously waiting for Longarm to speak first.

Longarm remained silent. During the years he'd worked out of the Denver office his cases had brought him into contact with several Indian tribes, including a number whose members had not yet learned English. Though the Digger language was not among those he had encountered, Longarm had a smattering of knowledge of half a dozen Indian languages, and had also learned more than a little bit about the sign language which was used by tribesmen to communicate with their fellows who shared no common tongue. He cudgeled his brain now, trying to decide which language might be understood by the Diggers and to summon up the right words to use.

When Longarm remained silent, the Indian finally said something that sounded like *"E-ee sai ee."*

Longarm recognized the words as being rooted in the Hopi tongue, of which he had only the smallest knowledge. However, he recognized the doubled "e-ee" as meaning "peace," and knew enough of universal Indian customs to reply in kind.

"E-ee sai ee," he repeated. Then he asked, "Talk English?"

Shaking his head, the Indian said something that sounded like *"Hakami."* His knitted brows and puzzled expression as well as the upward inflection of the word gave Longarm his clue.

"Long," he said, pointing to his own chest. Then he took out his wallet and flipped it open to show his badge.

Obviously the Indian was familiar with badges. He touched its raised insignia with a fingertip as though to assure himself it was really metal, then turned to his companions and said *"Ki-ha-chi."*

Longarm was still largely at sea. He was not sure the Indian was understanding him, though so far he had understood the gestures if not the language of the Digger. He tried again. Putting his hand on the rifle in his saddle scabbard he asked, "Apache?"

Shaking his head, the old man answered, "Apache *ni akami.*"

Longarm decided the Digger was telling him that the Apaches were nowhere close. Seeing that the effort to communicate with words wasn't working out, Longarm decided to try the universal sign language. He opened his hand wide, spreading his fingers. Holding it palm down, he made a sweeping gesture across his body, a sign of rejection. As he moved his hand he said one word, "Apache."

51

His face brightening, the old Digger nodded vigorously, to indicate that he had as little use for Apaches as the white man did. Then he repeated the sign Longarm had made and added a sweeping gesture that encompassed the village and its people.

"Apache *ni akami!*" he repeated. A murmur of voices rose from the group, and two of the older men nodded and one echoed the words "*ni akami.*"

Reasonably sure that he had interpreted the Indian's gestures and words correctly, as expressing dislike and perhaps even hatred for the Apaches, Longarm tried for more information. He tapped the butt of his holstered Colt, then lifted his hand, his forefinger extended to imitate a pistol-barrel, and flipped his thumb several times. Then he tapped his badge and his own chest and repeated the gesture that imitated the firing of a pistol.

Now the communication that had at last been established between Longarm and the Indian seemed to be working. The Digger nodded and smiled, but the smile quickly faded. His face grew solemn and he pointed to an oblong mound of earth, obviously a freshly filled grave, that rose a few paces apart from the huts.

"*Weh-yu,*" he said. Indicating the Indians behind him, he gestured toward Longarm's Colt and went on, "Apache *emuken.*"

This time Longarm did not understand whether the old headman's words and gestures meant that the body of an Apache or a Digger was in the grave. He reinforced his question by raising his eyebrows as he pointed toward the Indians grouped around the old man, then indicated the grave.

"Your people?" he asked.

Obviously, the headman did not understand Longarm's words, nor did he grasp the meaning of his gesture. He frowned for a moment, then pointed to the Colt at Longarm's hip, half-turned to the village man nearest him, and tapped his own chest.

"Apache," he said, raising his arm, his forefinger extended, his thumb cocked as though it was the hammer of a pistol. Crooking his thumb, he said a few quick words which

52

Longarm did not catch, but he understood when the man at whom the headman had gestured dropped to the ground.

Tapping his revolver butt, Longarm brought up his hand, his forefinger and thumb imitating the gesture the headman had made earlier.

"Apache shoot?" he asked.

Now the headman nodded vigorously, and Longarm understood that an Apache had killed whoever occupied the grave. Longarm swept his arm from north to south, and again questioned the headman by raising his eyebrows.

"Where Apache?" he asked.

Whether the Indian understood the gesture or the questioning look on Longarm's face, he got the message. Pointing first to the livery horse, then to the northeastern horizon, he brought his hand up until the finger pointed straight at the sky. Then he said, "Apache *haka.*"

Longarm interpreted the gesture and words as meaning that the Apache lived a half-day's ride to the northeast.

"How many?" he asked, holding out one hand and opening and closing his fingers, then tapping his fingertips with the tip of his other hand's forefinger.

Surprisingly, the headman understood Longarm's questioning gestures at once this time. He held up two fingers.

"Now, hold on!" Longarm said, his surprise so great that he forgot to use sign language. "You can't mean there's only two Apaches in—" Realizing what he was doing, Longarm quickly reverted to signs. Extending his hands with their palms turned upward, he shook his head. Then he closed his right hand, leaving his forefinger and index finger extended, while he gazed at the headman with his brows raised in questioning arcs.

Nodding vigorously, the headman stepped over to the group of Diggers and pulled a middle-aged woman and a young man from the group. He turned to Longarm again and gestured toward the woman, extending one finger, then added his index finger as he swivelled to point to the youth.

"A young fellow and a woman?" Longarm asked. Turning his head to look from one to the other. His question was directed as much to himself as it was to the headman, but the old

53

Digger got its drift and nodded emphatically again.

"Well, I got to admit that I can't figure this one out," Longarm said, more to himself than to the Indian. "And there's just one way to straighten it out. That's to ride on and see what I can find out for myself."

He had no way to thank the Diggers except to give them a friendly wave before he turned and started for his horse. The headman returned the wave as Longarm swung into the saddle and turned the livery horse in the direction the Indian had indicated.

Chapter 6

When Longarm left the little Digger settlement the sun was already high in the sky. It rose higher as he forged steadily ahead and the air grew hotter every minute as the blazing golden disc climbed on toward its zenith.

"If you'd had the sense God give a constipated jackass, old son, you'd've crawled into one of them little Digger huts and rested till evening, when it won't be so damn hot," he told himself under his breath. After shaking his head to force the drops of sweat to roll down his cheeks faster, he went on, "But maybe hunkering down in the shade wouldn't've helped all that much. In these parts there's just two kinds of summer weather, hot and hotter."

Ignoring the heat-created lure to urge his horse to move faster in order to stir up a breeze, he let the reins lie looped around his saddlehorn and lighted a cigar to keep himself awake as he continued to ride slowly ahead in the direction the Digger headman had indicated.

No two ways from Sunday about it, Longarm mused as he gazed ahead. *That writing fellow who calls himself Artemus*

Ward sure hit the bulls-eye when he said everybody talks about the weather, but nobody does anything about it. And you could give him another one to think about right now, old son, because you got an idea which way to head, but you don't know how far you're going to have to go to get there. In this country hereabouts there sure ain't no landmarks to guide a man.

Wherever Longarm looked, the vista was the same. He might as well have been riding across a boundless green ocean. Its only limit was the heat haze which his eyes could penetrate for three or four miles at most, while in a cooler country he'd have been able to see the usual seven to eight miles that marked the limit of vision for a man on horseback. Ahead and behind and all around, all that was visible was sagebrush. The low-growing plants filled the landscape in every direction, growing as high as the knees on the plodding legs of the livery horse.

There were no paths through the sage, and under the sun's blistering glare the tips of its branches were as motionless as though they had been painted on some huge, invisible canvas. The sky gave the same impression of being an artist's work. It was nearly blue along the line of the horizon, which only now and then could be seen through the ground haze. However, the hue of the vast canopy overhead grew progressively lighter until almost directly above his head it gathered around the glowing sun like a thin coat of molten gold.

Though by Longarm's standards he had slept well the night before, he found himself nodding in the saddle as the heat and monotony of the landscape worked their tricks. He lighted a fresh cheroot from the butt of the first to keep himself from dropping into a doze, and looked for some landmark ahead to keep from veering off to one side or the other in a country which really had no features to hold the attention of a rider.

At last he settled for holding the shadow cast by his horse on the leaf-tips of the low-growing sage and keeping the shadow at a uniform angle to the horse as it moved ahead. Even a slight straying by his horse from the straight line Longarm wanted to follow changed the shadow's form and alerted him to touch the reins and get back on his course. This worked well, and his heat-induced drowsiness faded now that he had something other than the problem of a case with no leads or clues to keep his mind busy.

At Longarm's first glimpse of the dust cloud approaching in front of him, his first thought was that the dust was raised by an Indian war-party. As he advanced and drew closer, the shimmer of the heat haze dancing above the ground diminished as the distance lessened. Even though their figures were still not fully distinct, he could see it was a wild mustang herd that was approaching, the hooves of the animals breaking the hard dry crust of the desert soil to create the dust that mingled with the ever-present heat haze.

In an automatic reaction to sighting the rising roiling cloud, Longarm had slid his Winchester out of its saddle scabbard and checked its loads. He was holding the rifle ready to shoulder it when the herd sighted and smelled him. The horses spooked at once and veered away. Only then did he see the animals clearly.

You got redskins on the brain, old son, Longarm scolded himself silently as he watched the mustangs streaming past, still a quarter of a mile distant. As he restored the Winchester to its sheath his thoughts ran on, *But this flat's where the Indians hereabouts come to catch their ponies, so maybe you wasn't all that much outa line getting ready to start shooting.*

Reining in, Longarm watched the mustang herd as it streamed past him. It was not a large herd, only thirty or forty animals, and the little horses were a mixed lot. A majority of them were smaller than the cowponies favored by ranchers, who like heft in their range mounts. There were some paints among them, and a dapple or two, but for the most part the horses were a solid reddish-brown, their streaming manes and tails a shade darker than their coats. Within a few minutes the herd passed and was soon hidden by its own dust cloud.

Looking at the motes of dust hanging thick in the windless air above the flat, Longarm decided to take his time in starting again. During his years of traveling on cases and chases, he'd lost his taste for the gritty prairie soil. He knew that the sun-shimmered dust cloud in the air ahead would clog his nostrils and coat his skin and creep into his mouth until its sourish, acrid dryness forced him to use more of his scanty supply of water than was wise. He was still lounging in his saddle when the crack of a rifle burst through the hazy air and a bullet sang by his hatbrim.

"Damned if this ain't getting to be an old story," he muttered, dropping once more from the horse's back to the ground.

As Longarm went down, he whipped his rifle from its scabbard again and carried it with him. He flexed his knees when his boot soles thunked on the baked soil and let the impetus given him by the jump carry him to his knees. When he settled down, kneeling, the tops of the sage reached halfway up his chest. Rifle shouldered, he squinted, peering through slitted eyelids, trying to pierce the veil of dust that still hung in the air.

Though he could see nothing, his invisible adversary apparently could. Another shot broke the stillness, but the slug whistled by above him. A thin blotch of powdersmoke forming a small, wispy wreath above the tops of the sagebrush gave Longarm the first clue he'd had of the location of his enemy.

Leveling the Winchester, aiming under the tops of the sagebrush below the wraith of gunsmoke, Longarm triggered off his shot. Before its echoes had died away, the shot drew a response. The aim of the rifleman concealed ahead was no better than it had been before. Though the slug cut through the tops of the sagebrush, it was wide of its mark, and missed both Longarm and the horse. The faint thunk of the bullet as it plowed into the ground half a dozen feet away barely reached his ears.

"Whoever that fellow is, he ain't such a much with a rifle," Longarm muttered. "But he might get off a lucky shot if he ain't stopped. Looks like you better start doing something about him, old son. The way he begun shooting, he'd be Apache by rights, but if he is he sure ain't got no horse, and there never was an Apache born that'd walk when he could ride. And there never was an Apache that didn't want another horse, either. Question is now, what's that fellow after? Me or the horse?"

As Longarm advanced slowly, crawling on all fours and pulling his rifle after him, he resisted the temptation to spring to his feet so that he could move faster. He also abandoned the idea of raising his head about the tops of the low-growing sagebrushes. He set his course by the angle of the shadows that the bushes cast on the hard yellow soil.

"It'd sure be nice if you could ride right up to that damn sniper, old son," he muttered under his breath as he stopped to give his knees a bit of rest from the grinding roughness of the sun-baked ground. "It'd be nice, but it'd be the easiest way you could pick out to get all shot up."

Well aware that the time he could give to thinking and planning was sharply limited, Longarm decided to risk another look. Before raising his head this time, he took a precaution that he'd learned to use early during his brushes with the Apaches in other areas of the West.

Taking off his hat, he angled the barrel of his Winchester back toward him and placed the hat on the rifle's muzzle. He made sure it would stay in position by bending the hat's leather sweatband out until he could hook it over the Winchester's front sight. Still lying down, but on his back this time, he lifted the rifle barrel until the hat's crown rose above the tops of the thick brushy sage.

His ruse drew an immediate response. No sooner had the hat cleared the sage than the hidden sniper's rifle cracked. The slug cut through the hot desert air and thudded into the hard ground a few inches from Longarm's side. Before the sharp sudden noise of the rifle's report had died away, a second shot followed the first. It bracketed the hat. The first slug had kicked up dust on the far side of the rifle butt; the second plowed up the hard soil between Longarm and the Winchester.

Had he been wearing the hat, the lead would have lodged in Longarm's body. Dropping the rifle below the tops of the brush, he wasted no time in scrambling as best he could without exposing himself into a new position a few feet away.

"He's Apache, all right," Longarm muttered, restoring his hat to his head. "Question is now, where's his horse? It stands

59

to reason the nag's got to be someplace close. And chances are that redskin's snaking over to it right now, to ride up and see if he's got a scalp to take."

Checking his horse's tether, Longarm filled his pockets with shells from his saddlebag and dropped belly-down. He began snaking ahead, propelling himself with his elbows and booted toes. His progress was painfully slow, for he knew that if the lurking Apache noticed any motion in the bushes, the Indian would send a few rifle slugs into the area where the brush was being disturbed.

Sheer common sense combined with his dislike for being a target warned Longarm to keep hidden as long as possible. He'd covered fewer than a dozen yards in his slow, cautious advance when the drumming of hoofbeats broke the desert's stillness. He swung his head, trying to locate by their sound the point from which the hoofbeats were coming, but they seemed to fill the air. At last he gave up the effort.

"He's a cagey one," Longarm muttered. "And all you can do right now is outguess him. Let him get so close to that livery cayuse that all he'll be thinking about is getting his hands on the reins. Then he won't be paying much mind to you, and you'll have a chance to get off the first shot, because it's likely that's the only shot that's going to count."

Holding his cover, Longarm listened to the drumming raised on the otherwise silent prairie by the unshod hooves of his adversary's horse. The Apache remained silent, though the hoofbeats of his mount enabled Longarm to keep track of his location. He heard the drumming beats pass his hiding place and swivelled to keep his face turned toward the Indian.

Suddenly the hoofbeats stopped. Longarm took the silence as his cue. Rifle ready, he rose to his knees. The Apache had reined in beside the livery horse. In the instant that passed while Longarm corrected his aim, he got his first clear view of his adversary. The Indian was swinging off his own mount, his back toward Longarm. He had on a battered leather vest and the kind of denim jeans worn by white ranchers. A headband was around his jet-black shoulder-length hair.

For the space of two breaths, Longarm held his fire; the idea of backshooting a man was repugnant to him. Then the

Indian turned to slide to the ground and Longarm got a brief glimpse of white under the dark leather jacket. The Apache saw Longarm and lurched to fall sidewise across his pony as Longarm's rifle slug whistled above him.

While Longarm was levering a fresh shell into his rifle's chamber, the Indian pony spurted off with a leap and settled at once into a hoof-drumming gallop. Swinging his rifle muzzle, Longarm tried for a shot at the Apache, who still hung sideways over his mount's back. Longarm got a glimpse of a leg lifted to be thrown across the back of the galloping pony, and knew that even with the best possible luck all he could hope for was inflicting a minor wound on the retreating Apache.

Longarm lowered his Winchester and began running toward his horse. The Apache was still cutting a shuck across the sagebrush-covered prairie by the time Longarm got to his own mount and swung into his saddle. He kicked the horse ahead, his eyes fixed on the fleeing Indian. The man's horse was obviously still fresh, for it was already growing small in the distance by the time Longarm spurred it on the Apache's trail.

Longarm kept the galloping Apache pony in sight until it disappeared below the ledge of another of the downslopes that marked the prairie. Though he did not slacken his pace, there was no sign of the fleeing man when he reached the long decline that stretched ahead until the details of the virtually featureless landscape became invisible beneath the heat haze.

Puffing out a long breath of disgust, Longarm reined his mount to a walk. He took out a cigar and brought a match to life with his thumbnail as he studied the long, gentle treeless slope which dipped in front of him. The light breeze that earlier had blown fitfully for a few moments was gone now.

"You sure done the wrong thing this time, old son," he scolded himself aloud. "Letting that Apache get away like you did is just the same as killing him. Either way, he ain't going to do no talking. Only good thing that come outa the little dustup is that now you got tracks to follow."

Smoke from his cheroot trailed behind him, hanging for a few moments in the windless air as Longarm began following the trail left by the Indian's pony. The Apache had not been able to take the time necessary to cover his horse's tracks. The sage thinned a few hundred yards beyond the point where the Indian had been when Longarm fired at him, and the hoof-prints of his pony were clear and easy to follow, the only tracks that broke the soil's dry brittle surface.

For the first mile of his flight, the Apache had kept his mount at a gallop, the hoofprints forming wide-spaced parallel pairs, forefeet and hindfeet close together in a span half again as long as the mustang's body. Then the prints veered off at a sharp angle, and Longarm saw why as he reined his horse to follow them. Ahead, the level desert terrain was broken by the ragged edge of a wide crevasse.

Drawing closer to the undulating rim of the winding gulch, Longarm saw the freshly broken earth where the Apache had reined his horse into the deep, wide gully. Its bottom was lined with bright sand, so light in hue that it was almost white. The sand bore no vegetation, and the steeply sloped side showed a wide swathe of disturbed dirt where the Indian had slid his mount to the sandy bottom.

Longarm wasted no time in reining his horse down the path his fleeing quarry had taken. The livery mount balked for a moment, then hunkered down and slid to the bottom, where it regained its usual stance with an unhappy snort. Longarm did not urge the horse along the bottom of the ravine at once, but sat for a moment studying the hoofprints in the level expanse of off-white sand that covered the floor of the miniature valley.

Eastward, to his right, the hoofprints of the Apache's pony dimpled the soft level surface. The hoofprint pattern changed almost at once. Now the crescent-shaped depressions which had been cut by the pony's galloping hooves became full prints. Even the twin heel-calks were plainly marked in the smooth yielding surface of the sun-baked sand. The prints were no longer spaced in pairs, but formed the staggered pattern made by the hooves of a walking horse.

Longarm nodded with satisfaction. "He figured he'd give you the slip when he got down here," he said into the stillness of the breezeless air. "And it just might be that's what he's done, old son. Too bad you never did get a good look at him.

He might just be the Apache Kid, and if he was it'd sure save you a lot of looking. There ain't but one way to find out, so you better get moving. As long as there's a decent trail, that redskin ain't going to find it all that easy to shake away."

Twitching the reins, Longarm toed his mount into motion again. The animal had gotten its breath back by now, and it moved steadily along the sandy floor of the winding gulch. As he rode, the sun at his back, casting his own shadow and that of the horse ahead of him, Longarm kept his eyes on the hoofprints he was following while he turned over in his mind the job that still lay ahead.

"You sure got your job cut out for you, old son," he said to himself around the stub of the cigar that he still held clenched between his teeth. "If it ain't the Apache Kid you're trailing after, how in hell are you going to locate him in this damn empty place?"

Contemplating the possibility that he might spend days crisscrossing the wild, trackless expanse of Frenchman Flat, he kept his eyes on the hoof-pocks that dotted the sandy bottom of the dry wash as the horse plodded patiently ahead. After another mile or so, still chewing on the stub of his dead cigar, he came back to the thought that had occurred to him earlier, but which he had discarded as being too improbable to be realistic.

Now, you mighta been wrong when you got the idea the first time, old son, he mused. But there can't be too many Apaches left around that'll shoot first and ask questions afterwards, and this fellow you're trailing has got to have some reason for sniping you. Course, it might be he's just one of them mean Apaches who hates the guts of every white man that crosses his path. But if it is the Kid up ahead, you sure got a long leg up on him, because sooner or later he's going to have to stop, and that's when you'll catch up to him.

In the little meandering ravine through which he was riding, the shadow of its western wall had continued its slow creeping progress across the sandy floor as Longarm's horse plodded along patiently. The hoofprints in the sand-covered floor no longer stood out in sharp relief in the gathering dusk, and he touched the reins to slow his horse a bit, not wanting to miss a spot where his quarry might have scrambled up the gully's wall.

Ahead, the wall of the gully curved gently. Since his McClellan saddle had no horn, Longarm had tucked the ends of his slack reins under one thigh, where he could get to them without having to grope. He reached for them now, since experience had taught him that sudden drop-offs and other horsemen's hazards might lie beyond even a gentle curve in a wide, deep canyon's walls.

He had entered the arc by now, glancing idly at the sheer walls which suddenly rose on each side as the desert sands gave way to rock. Then he turned his eyes ahead again and what he saw made him pull back hard on the reins and reach with his free hand for his rifle butt.

Across the canyon floor not more than fifty yards distant was a solid line of mounted Indians.

Chapter 7

Longarm's right hand darted toward the stock of his rifle. His move was one of instinct, and he caught himself before his fingers had closed around the Winchester. Even as he was recovering from his surprise at the unexpected sight of the Indians, he saw that none of them had weapons in their hands. Though all but a few carried rifles in fringed buckskin saddle scabbards, not one of them had made a move to grasp a gunstock.

Reining in, Longarm raised his right arm, elbow bent, the palm of his hand outward, fingertips to the sky, in the universal sign of peace.

Near the center of the line, one of the Indians replied with the same gesture. Suppressing a sigh of relief and letting his upraised hand fall to his side, Longarm sat and waited for the Indians to make the first move. He did not have long to wait. The man who had replied to his peace sign dug a moccasin-clad heel into his pony's flank and the animal started forward. Longarm nudged his own horse with the toe of his boot and advanced to meet him.

When only a yard or more separated the two horses, the Indian squeezed his knees together on his mount's barrel. When the animal halted, Longarm reined in. Many times in the past he had gone through the ritual ceremony of a first meeting with strange Indians, and he was determined not to be the first to speak. To break the silence first, even though all he said was his name, would have put him into an inferior position in the eyes of the Indian leader.

Facing him, the red man was equally silent. The two stared expressionlessly at each other, both as motionless as statues. When he felt that enough time had passed to establish himself as an equal to the Indian leader, Longarm moved. He held his hand in the peace gesture for a moment, then slid a pair of cigars from his vest pocket. Being careful to hold the cigars in his left hand, Longarm put one in his mouth, and took the other in his right hand before leaning forward in his saddle to offer the cigar to the Indian.

For a moment the bronzed face of the tribesman remained frozen and motionless. Then he nodded and reached forward, taking the cigar. Longarm extracted a match and flicked it into life with a quick scrape of his thumbnail. He extended the hand holding the match toward the Indian. As the other man leaned forward to reach the burning match, Longarm matched his motion and the two puffed the tobacco into life at the same time.

As he removed the cigar from his mouth after inhaling deeply of the fragrant smoke, the Indian spoke at last. Tapping his chest with his forefinger, he said, "Mururi."

Longarm nodded and tapped his own chest. "Long," he said. "Deputy United States marshal."

Mururi did not reply at once, and as the silence continued Longarm realized that he was being tested by the Indian protocol or custom common to all tribes except the lowly Diggers or the so-called "civilized" tribes that were slowly being resettled in Indian Territory. The western tribes which still roamed free clung to the old ways.

Longarm understood enough of Indian attitudes to realize that the first to break the silence would lose face. He waited, trying to think of a way to resume talking, and at last decided on a question that would allow him to resume the conversation without lowering himself in the Indian leader's eyes.

Indicating with a nod the Indians lined up beyond Mururi, he asked, "Ute?"

Mururi shook his head, "Chemihuevi," he replied.

Longarm recognized the tribal name, though he had heard it only a few times before. The Chemihuevis were akin to the Utes, one of several minor tribes that at some point now lost in time had separated from the main body to establish their own culture. His strategy had succeeded, at least in part. Now the conversation could be resumed. He swept his arm in a gesture that took in the territory from the southeast north and then to the southwest.

"Chemihuevi range?" he asked.

Again Mururi shook his head. "Horse range. Peace land. We not fight here. All come, take horses."

Longarm nodded that he understood, as indeed he did. Before the days when white buffalo hunters invaded the prairies east of the Rockies the Indians had established such common hunting grounds at a number of points on the vast plains.

In the buffalo range that once had extended from a few miles north of the Gulf of Mexico to above the Canadian border, even the fierce and territorially jealous Comanches recognized the right of the other tribes to hunt peacefully when the vast herds strayed into Comanche territory during their endless cycle of migration. It did not matter that some of these tribes, perhaps most of them were those with which the Comanches shared undying enmity; their right to hunt temporarily on Comanche territory was respected.

"Where Apaches?" Longarm asked.

For a moment the Indian sat in motionless silence, as if debating whether or not to reply. Then he pointed to the northeast and swept his arm in a short arc north to south.

"Apache," he replied, then gestured in shorter arcs. "Lipan. Paiute."

"What about the Diggers?" Longarm asked.

For a moment Mururi stared expressionlessly. Then he shook his head and shrugged, the corners of his mouth turned down. His face and gesture needed no interpretation. Longarm understood without them that the Chemihuevi chief was in effect saying, "Who cares?"

Another long moment of silence followed. Then Mururi asked, "You iron horse man?"

Longarm shook his head. He took out his wallet and flipped it open to show his marshal's badge. When Mururi had finished examining it, his brows drawn together in a thoughtful frown, Longarm pointed to the east and said, "United States law. I guess you know about that?"

"*Na* bureau?" the Indian asked.

Longarm shook his head.

"*Na* railroad?" Mururi persisted.

"No," Longarm replied. "You don't like the railroad, I take it?" he asked.

Mururi's only response was a tightening of his lips.

When Longarm saw that the Indian was not going to answer, he borrowed the word he'd just heard Mururi use. "*Na* railroad," he said, emphasizing his words with a negative headshake. "Law. Hunt bad man."

"Bad man Indian?"

For a split second Longarm debated whether to answer or to remain silent. Then he recalled how information was circulated in some mysterious fashion between Indians of all tribes, and nodded.

"Bad Apache," he told the Chemihuevi chief. "Maybe you know him?"

Mururi's expression did not change, nor did he reply at once. At last he broke his silence. "You trade?" he asked.

Now it was Longarm's turn to be silent. Though he did not allow his puzzlement to show in his expression, he wondered at once what the Chemihuevi chief would ask in return for information about the Apache Kid.

"Maybe you better tell me what kind of trade you got in mind," he suggested.

"You *na* railroad, *na* Indian Bureau," Mururi replied. "So who you are?"

"Law," Longarm said after trying vainly to find another way of describing his job to the Indian.

"Law chief?" Mururi asked.

Longarm shook his head. "I ain't no chief." He looked beyond Mururi at the Chemihuevi Indians who were still sitting their horses, their faces expressionless, as they watched him and their chief. Gesturing at the line of Indians with a wave of his hand, he said, "Just a plain fighting man, like them."

If Mururi was disappointed, he did not show it. His face still displayed the tight-lipped stoicism that betrayed nothing.

"Railroad chief *na* do like you say?" he asked at last.

Once more Longarm shook his head, then said slowly, "I can't boss the railroad men, Mururi. Why do you ask me that?"

"*Na* good, railroad. Scare mustangs. Mustangs go, *na* horse for people."

"That's your people you're talking about? The Chemihuevis?"

"All people. Railroad come, *na* horse Chemihuevi, *na* horse Apache, *na* horse Paiute."

"If I get your meaning, all the Indians hereabouts hunt these horses on Frenchman Flat, then."

Struggling with the unfamiliar words, Mururi frowningly repeated, "Fra-ma-fla?"

Speaking slowly, Longarm repeated, "Frenchman Flat," while he swept his arm in a wide arc to indicate that he was talking about the area surrounding them.

Mururi's frown cleared away. He pointed to Longarm and imitated the gesture he'd just seen, then nodded and said, "You say 'Fra-ma-fla.' Chemihuevi say *na-ko-lo.*"

"But they mean the same place," Longarm agreed. He could almost feel the lessening of the tension that had hung between him and the Indian leader as they reached their first clear understanding. He went on, "All tribes catch horses here?"

"All horse people." Mururi nodded. "Chemihuevi. Apache. Paiute." He shook his head and then repeated, "Railroad come, horse go."

For some time now the suspicion had grown on Longarm that the chief knew a great deal more English than he wanted to admit. He decided to test his theory and at the same time play on the long-standing dislike and distrust that almost every Indian tribe felt for the Apaches in order to get the information he needed.

"You feel like making a trade, Mururi?" he asked.

"How trade?"

When Longarm replied, he abandoned the pidgin English. "Tell me where I can find the Apache I'm after," he said. "You do that and I'll see if I can get the railroad folks to put their tracks around Frenchman Flat."

"They do this thing if you tell them so?" Mururi asked.

For a fleeting moment Longarm was tempted to give Mururi the assurance he was asking, but his lifetime habit of sticking to the truth prevailed. He shook his head slowly.

"Now, I can't make no promise like that," he frowned, speaking slowly to avoid any possibility of being misunderstood. "I don't run nothing where them folks that're building the railroad is concerned."

"You are not chief among them?"

"Not by a long shot. But I done a favor or two for the man that's putting up the money, and he's brought me a long ways to get me here so I can help him, which is what I'm trying to do."

"And if you help him, he will help you." Mururi nodded. "This is what you tell me now?"

"That's about the size of it," Longarm agreed. "But all I can guarantee you is that he'll listen real careful, and maybe he'll agree when I tell him why you don't want the railroad busting up the country where you and the other tribes gets your horse stock."

"It is enough that you tell him and that he listens. If he is indeed your friend, he will do as you ask." Mururi frowned thoughtfully as he spoke.

Even though the Chemihuevi chieftain tried to his keep voice flat and expressionless, Longarm could see that the Indian was pleased with the offer. He also realized clearly now that Mururi understood a great deal more English than he had revealed during their earlier conversation.

"I ain't promising nothing, Mururi," Longarm warned.

"Like I told you, all I come here for was to catch up with whoever's been sniping at the railroad men that're doing the survey. But I can sure try."

Mururi did not speak for several moments, but instead gazed intently at Longarm, who tried to ignore the Apache's obsidian eyes. When at last he did speak, Mururi uttered only one short word.

"Te-lo," he said, gesturing toward the east. "You say Apache Kid."

"That's where he's holed up?" Longarm asked. He kept his voice level, hiding satisfaction at getting the information.

"Te-lo," the Indian repeated, nodding as he spoke. "Mother, she *Te-gra.* You say she Apache Annie."

Longarm kept a straight face in spite of his surprise at the sudden ability of Mururi to speak reasonably good English. It was not the first time he'd encountered an Indian who had at first pretended not to understand the white man's language, and later had proved to have a reasonably good command of it. Since his luck had been good so far, he decided to push for more.

"I guess you know where they are?" he asked very casually, as though the information meant little to him.

Mururi hesitated for a moment, then nodded. His face was still expressionless. He pointed down the canyon in the direction Longarm had been traveling.

"Mebbeso there," he said.

"There? Along the canyon?"

Nodding again, the Chemihuevi repeated his gesture.

"How far?" Longarm asked.

Mururi lifted his shoulders in a half-shrug, but made no other reply.

"A day's ride?" Longarm persisted. "Two days?"

Mururi shook his head and said, "Mebbeso sun go down you not get there."

"All the same, I guess I better be moving," Longarm told the Indian. "I got enough water in my canteen to carry me till tomorrow. You know where there's a water hole anyplace along the way?"

71

"You see before dark," Mururi replied. He raised his hand and gestured toward the canyon in the direction he'd told Longarm to take. "Look good, you see."

Longarm nodded and said, "Thanks, Mururi. Now, remember I ain't made no promise that I'll have much luck getting the railroad not to run right down the middle of the flat, but I'll do the best I can."

Mururi showed neither pleasure nor disappointment. With a nod, he reined his horse around and started back toward his band. Longarm watched him for a moment, then nudged his own mount ahead. He let the horse set its own pace as he continued down the sandy floor of the wide canyon.

Although the day had been well along by the time Longarm resumed his journey after his encounter with Mururi and the Chemihuevis, it seemed to him that the sun would never set. The blazing orb appeared to hang motionless, sending its hot rays into the deep sand that lay in a deep coat across the floor of the wide valley.

Although the terrain's gentle downslope should have made the going easier, the livery horse seemed to find it progressively harder to lift its hooves from the surface that was swallowing them almost to the fetlock with each plodding step forward. Long before the sun dropped below the rim of the wide crevasse, the horse was moving forward with all the speed of a weary snail, its head drooping a bit lower as each minute ticked away.

Old son, Longarm mused as he stared at the gentle sloping walls of the wide crevasse, *If this damned nag moves much slower, you're going to be run over by a snail, if snails can live hereabouts without melting down plumb to a grease spot. But that redskin said there's water up ahead, even if you ain't come to it yet. And with an empty canteen and a thirsty horse, you need that water sooner instead of after a while.*

Even at the distance of more than a mile, Longarm spotted the spring when at last it came into sight. Head-high on the slanting valley wall, a streak of green stretched down to the sandy floor. The horse must have smelled the water or sensed its nearness with the mysterious perception given to animals.

It pricked up its ears and increased its pace a bit. Then, as its slow advance brought it closer to the green spot, it tossed its head and whinnied and would have broken into a gallop except for the pressure of Longarm's firm hand on the reins.

"Just take it easy now," Longarm commanded. His voice sounded raspy to him as he spoke, even though he'd been taking small sips from the canteen as the day waned. "We come about as far today as a man and his horse oughta try in country like this. Once we get up to that spring, both of us is going to have a good drink and a long night's rest."

After he'd reined in beside the green swathe on the canyon wall and dismounted, he did not allow the animal to drink until he had led it firmly away from the small pool for several minutes and its sides had stopped heaving.

Although it seemed a long while before he reached the spring with its welcome spot of green, the time lapse was a matter of minutes, not hours. The sun had seemed to decline faster during the last few miles he'd covered. Its rays no longer reached the valley floor, but had climbed the eastern wall of the canyon almost to its rim. The sky above was now clear of haze and in the east it was darkening with the promise of nightfall.

He let the horse take several swallows from the little pool the spring formed on the canyon floor. The pool was small enough for Longarm to have spanned with both thumbs touching and his fingers spread. It had no outlet. The dry, sterile sand absorbed what water did not evaporate in the sun's heat, and the water in the pool had a slight tinge of salt when Longarm tasted it before letting his horse drink. But when he held his cupped hand in the tiny stream that trickled down the canyon wall and tasted that, he found the water pure and sweet.

Longarm was careful to pull his mount's head away from the pool before it could drink enough to make it founder. The horse neighed unhappily and tossed its head, but Longarm kept his grip on the reins and held it away again, then repeated the process twice more before he judged the thirsty animal had taken enough to last it for a short while.

He tethered the animal a short distance away from the pool. The sunlight showed above the canyon's rim only as a knife blade of brightness and the floor itself was in deep shadow that promised darkness soon. After drinking from his cupped hand, Longarm filled his empty canteen. Then he hunkered down and lighted a cigar.

By now the sunlight had left most of the sky in the suddenness of a desert sunset. Only a fringe of deepening reddish light outlined the canyon wall. Longarm did not quite believe his eyes when he saw the tiny trickle of smoke rising against the darkening sky above the canyon's rim less than a mile ahead. He blinked twice, but the ghostly finger of wavering white did not vanish.

"Looks like you've found the place Mururi told you was here, old son," he said in a half-whisper. "That's got to be the place where the Apache Kid and his mama are holed up. And, soon as it gets dark enough, it won't be much of a trick to slip along down there and surprise 'em with a little visit."

Chapter 8

Longarm's years as a lawman had taught him many things, among them the need to be patient. Though he was sure the smoke ahead marked the hideout of the Apache Kid and his mother, Apache Annie, he pushed away the urge to hurry down the canyon and confirm his suspicions. There were other matters which needed his attention, and time to take care of them before darkness fell.

His legs ached with the saddle cramp that always comes with long hours on horseback, his empty stomach demanded food, and he needed a bit of time to consider his next moves and plan his course of action. Daylight was still lingering, and Longarm knew that his best chance to make a successful foray would come during the hours of darkness.

Taking his necessary pouch out of his saddlebag, Longarm stepped over to the base of the sloping canyon wall and hunkered down. He took out the two soft leather pouches of emergency rations that were in the bag, and after scanning the canyon floor quickly he settled in a sitting position. Stretching out his long legs, he leaned back and chewed patiently on jerky and parched corn while he waited for nightfall.

Darkness was not long in coming. Though he had spent a lot of time in the high desert country, Longarm was still not quite accustomed to the swift transition in a country that moved almost instantly from twilight to darkness. It seemed to him that he had no sooner settled down than the night sky filled the open gap above the canyon and stars suddenly dotted it with the brilliance of so many diamonds, the thin air seeming to bring them close enough to touch. Still Longarm did not move. The darkness was not quite full yet, and he saw no need to hurry.

When his eyes could no longer make out each bump and hump on the sand-covered canyon floor, Longarm stirred. His horse had been standing long enough to be fresh again, and was beginning to stamp restlessly. Longarm stood up and led the animal to the little pool that had now been refilled by the trickling spring. He took a few swallows of the cool clear water that cascaded down the sloping wall and let the horse drink from the pool at its base. Then he gathered the reins in his hand and led the horse toward the place where he had seen the tiny trickle of smoke.

His footsteps and the soft thudding of his horse's hooves were almost inaudible as they moved along the soft yielding sand. Even at a slow, unhurried pace, only a few minutes passed before Longarm could see a faint glow of light spilling across the canyon floor. The intensity of the glow increased as he drew closer, and soon he saw the arch of the cave from which the light came outlined in the canyon wall.

"Gypsum cave," Longarm muttered under his breath. "More'n likely that's where the Apache Kid and his mama has set up housekeeping. Nice and dry and clean, and water not too far off. Be the kind of place I'd look for, too, was I in their shoes. But it's a little bit soon to pay 'em a call, old son. Find a safe place to put the horse, then mosey on back and wait till they settle down and go to bed."

There was no noise coming from the cave, but Longarm took no chances in disturbing its occupants. He swung to the far side of the canyon floor, moving slowly to break the

76

rhythm of the horse's hoofbeats, and led the animal down the wash until he found a break in its high wall. The niche was a small one, but deep enough to back the animal into.

Although Longarm was sure the well-trained livery mount would stand, he chose not to risk leaving the possibility to chance. A few hard kicks with the heel of his boot broke off a chunk of the stone-hard soil from the rim of the little opening. When he wrapped the reins around it and laid it on the ground, the heavy chunk became an effective temporary tether.

From force of habit, Longarm reached for the Winchester in its saddle scabbard. He had drawn it halfway out when he remembered how short he was of ammunition. Then it occurred to him that the long gun would be more hindrance than help if the cave was small. With a shrug, he slid the rifle back into its sheath and started retracing his steps to the gypsum cave.

He entered the rough arched opening silently, blinking as his night-contracted pupils adjusted to the light that poured around a jutting shoulder. As his visual capacity increased he could see that the entryway stretched almost twenty feet in a straight line before opening out into what must be a fairly large chamber. Directly ahead he could see two unsaddled horses, but the light that seeped into the entrance was out of sight in the section of the cave's main chamber, which he guessed must open almost at right angles to the entry.

He continued his slow advance, planting each foot solidly on rough corrugations of the stone-hard floor before putting his weight on it. After he had moved eight or ten feet from the entryway, he began to hear small noises ahead, the faint click of metal against metal, and the occasional soft scraping of boot soles on the cave's stonelike floor.

When a man's voice broke the silence, Longarm stopped and froze in place. The speaker was using a language unfamiliar to Longarm, but he guessed it to be one of the several tribal dialects of the Apache tongue. After a moment the man fell silent and a woman's voice, throatier and a bit softer, took up the conversation.

Using the noise made by the speakers to mask any sounds he might make and hoping the horses would not betray his

77

presence by whinnying or stamping, Longarm advanced quickly to cover the eight or ten feet that took him to the edge of the cave's wall where it widened into the larger chamber he had deduced lay beyond the entrance.

When he reached the edge and stopped, the conversation in the hidden section of the cavern was still going on. From the emphatic manner in which the participants were speaking, Longarm got the idea that he was listening to an argument. He took off his wide-brimmed hat and peered around the corner of the wall.

The underground chamber beyond the cave's entryway was a large one, an irregular cavern roughly oval in shape, perhaps thirty or thirty-five feet in its long dimension and a bit more than twenty feet wide. The top of the opening rose ten feet above Longarm's head, and the whiteness of the cave's gypsum walls and smooth level floor with their compacted alabaster-white granules reflected brilliantly and even seemed to amplify the light of the single lantern that stood on an upended wooden box near its center.

Longarm paid little attention to the two desert ponies that stood with their heads to the wall just past the point where the cave began to widen. They were unsaddled, the saddles on the floor a few feet past them. Two crumpled heaps of blankets made untidy sprawls on the floor near the arcing wall that curved away from the entry. A rifle leaned against the wall beside each of the bedrolls. There were several boxes and a small keg in the narrow end of the wall beyond the fire. Near them lay a towsack, its top open, spilling out lumps of charcoal. Cloth-wrapped bundles secured by leather thongs had been tossed down in no apparent order in the area beyond the coal sack.

Longarm took passing notice of these objects as he swept his eyes in a quick scanning of the cave. He was more interested in the pair seated near the end of the cavern. An iron pot was between them, a skillet balanced across its top. Wisps of smoke were rising around the skillet from the charcoal that burned in the pot.

Longarm noted the cooking arrangement only in passing. His attention was concentrated on the oddly paired couple.

They were fishing chunks of meat out of the skillet with the tips of their knives, occasionally stopping between bites to talk for a moment or two in the guttural Apache tongue.

He had seen the man earlier in the day, and exchanged shots with him on Frenchman Flat, but his glimpses then had been fleeting and from a distance. Now he recognized the Indian at once as the Apache Kid, whom he'd arrested once several years earlier. Though he had never seen the woman before, she had the same kind of broad square face, wide flattened nose, and heavy jaw that marked the Kid's features. Longarm knew that she must be the Kid's mother, Apache Annie, for it was impossible to miss or ignore the family similarities.

There was also a resemblance in the way they were dressed. The Apache Kid had on tightly fitted buckskin trousers and a pullover shirt or jacket of rough brown duck. A gunbelt was buckled around his waist, the birdshead grip of a New Line Colt protruding from its holster. He wore his hair long, almost to his shoulders, held in place with a faded blue bandana folded into a strip as a headband.

Annie wore either buckskin trousers or leggings under her long billowing calico skirt. Her blouse was of the same brown duck from which her son's was made, but it was cut fuller and buttoned down the front. A wide leather belt ornamented with several oval *conchos* was pulled tightly around her full waist, and her hair, which showed no traces of gray, was caught up with a narrow leather headband which had a single small silver *concho* centered in front.

Since Longarm's last look at him, the Kid had aged. That look had been six years ago, when the Kid was being taken from the courtroom in Carson City to begin a life sentence in Nevada's notoriously tough prison. He had been sentenced to life imprisonment for the murder of a guard who was accompanying a shipment of gold ingots heading for the assay office in the state capital.

Looking at him now, Longarm could see that prison life had not been kind to the Apache Kid. His obsidian-black eyes glistened through slitted lids in the yellow lanternlight. Deep lines ran from the edges of his nostrils down to the corners of his puffy lips, and a scar that Longarm did not remember formed a jagged line on one of his high cheekbones. Lumps of muscle rolled at the corners of his wide jaws as he chewed his food.

Finishing his scrutiny of the Kid, Longarm returned his attention to Apache Annie. The resemblance between mother and son was unmistakable. Except for the difference in their ages, and Annie's unscarred face, she and the Kid could have been cast from the same mold. Annie's nose was flat and her nostrils wide-splayed. Her lips were fuller than the Kid's, and the lines from her nostrils to the corners of her mouth were deeper.

Well, you got the Kid cornered again, old son, Longarm told himself silently as he watched the pair eating and exchanging an occasional remark in their native language. *Or maybe it's the other way around, seeing he knows the lay of the land better'n you do.*

Longarm's train of thought was interrupted by some kind of disagreement between the Kid and Annie which caused them to raise their voices and talk at the same time. Even if Longarm had been able to translate what they were saying, he would have had trouble understanding the guttural Apache words that poured from both of them at the same time.

As he studied the two Apaches and their belongings strewn around on the floor of the cave, Longarm could see no way of taking them by surprise. He had learned from his first encounter with the Apache Kid that the Indian paid no attention to the odds against him when facing an adversary. On that occasion the Kid had started to draw while looking down the muzzle of Longarm's revolver, and the Apache had almost managed to trigger off a shot before the Colt's slug tore into his shoulder and ended his effort to break free.

Might be the best thing you can do is slip away right now, old son. Longarm frowned as he continued his silent monologue. *Get outside the cave and move a little ways down the draw, where you can wait without 'em spotting you for 'em to come out and do their business before they go to bed. There sure ain't no pot in here for 'em to use, or you'd've smelled it.*

And if they start outside before you move away, there ain't a chance in the world that they'd miss spotting you.

Before he'd reached a decision, the argument between Annie and the Kid became louder and more heated, and soon they were shouting.

Longarm had no further need to debate with himself whether to go or stay. The raised voices of the Kid and Annie would cover any slight noise that he might make in leaving the cavern. He stepped back carefully and started to turn around. Before he could finish his move a hard prod in his back froze him in place, for he recognized the feeling instantly. The object pressing between his shoulder blades was the muzzle of a gun.

"All right, whoever you are," he said quickly, trying to get the words out before the gun-toter could pull the trigger. "I ain't fool enough to try nothing or to argufy when I got a gun shoved in my backbone. Just tell me what to do."

"Stand real still, for openers," the man holding the gun replied. "Soon as I relieve you of that Colt you're carrying, I'll feel better about taking a closer look at you."

Longarm felt a hand grasp the butt of his revolver and lift it from his holster. He stood motionless, waiting for the man to search him further, but his captor did not bother to look for other weapons.

"Now march on in to where the Kid and Annie can get a look at you," the man ordered. "It might be they know you better'n I do, seeing you was so all-fired interested in snooping around here listening to 'em."

Before Longarm could move, he heard a crash followed by the scuffing of moccasin-clad feet from the cave. The Apache Kid appeared in the passageway, his own revolver drawn. He glanced at Longarm and his eyes narrowed with hatred. They widened when he turned them on the man whose gun was still pressing into Longarm's back.

"You've caught yourself a good one, Dorsey," he told the man. "That fellow you're covering is a man I got a big score to settle with. I swapped shots with him this morning, only then I didn't get close enough to him to see who he was."

"You throwed down on him even when you didn't know who you was shooting at?" The man addressed as Dorsey frowned. "I ain't sure the boss would like that."

"Let the boss tell me about it, then," the Apache Kid said curtly. "How the hell was I to know? I figured he was one of them railroad surveyors we're supposed to stop. Now that I see him up close, I know who he is. He's a U.S. marshal that works outa Denver. His name's Long, but mostly he's called Longarm."

"Well, I'll be a son of a bitch!" Dorsey exclaimed. "I figured when I seen him watching you that he was somebody trying to make trouble for us, but I didn't know who he was. Sure, I've heard a lot of the boys cuss Longarm, but this is the first time I ever seen him."

Annie arrived in time to hear Dorsey's closing words. She was carrying one of the rifles Longarm had seen leaning against the wall of the cave.

"Looks like you got here about the right time, Dorsey," she said. "Me and the boy didn't have no idea that this fellow was snooping around. And we was just talking about you, wondering when you'd show up."

"I don't recall setting no special time, Annie," Dorsey replied. "Figured you'd know I'd show up after I'd told you I was going to."

Longarm had remained silent while Dorsey and the Apaches were talking, but his mind had been working at top speed. He was still holding his hands above his head, and he used them as an excuse to start getting the edge he needed to break away from the trio.

"Seeing as how all three of you've got guns on me and you've already took away my pistol, I don't guess you'll mind if I let my hands hang down natural," he said. "My arms is getting just a little bit stiff, holding 'em up over my head this way."

"You're going to be a hell of a lot stiffer all over before we get through with you," Dorsey told him. "From what I've heard about you, you're a right cagey bastard, Long. You keep them hands up till we figure out the best way to get rid of you."

82

"There's just one way of getting rid of him that I'm interested in," the Apache Kid said, turning to face Dorsey. "And it ain't shooting. That's too easy. I owe this son of a bitch a lesson, damn him! He's the one that caught up with me and put me in the pen. I'd still be there if I hadn't broke out!"

"What you got in mind?" Dorsey asked.

"I aim to do some carving on him, like us Apaches used to do in the old days. When I get through with him we'll haul his carcass out on the flat and put it where them surveyors is sure to find him."

"That oughta make 'em lose their stomach for working on the railroad line," Apache Annie broke in. "And that's what your boss is after, ain't it?"

"Sure," Dorsey nodded. "But carving up somebody Apache-style's just a little bit strong for me."

"Who asked you to help?" the Kid demanded. "I'm the one Longarm put in prison. This is between me and him!"

"I still ain't so sure the boss would like it," Dorsey told the Apaches.

Longarm had been listening to the conversation between the thug and the Apaches and not really liking what he heard. Now he saw a chance to buy time, if he could drive a wedge between them.

"I ain't sure your boss would like it either, Dorsey," he broke in. "The man that's putting down that railroad line's got enough friends in Washington to get soldiers sent over here clear from Fort Wingate to guard the work crews if you start doing a lot of killing."

"Shut up, Longarm!" the Apache Kid snapped. "This ain't your game no longer. Annie and me are the ones that'll be telling Dorsey and his friends what to do. One way or the other, I'm going to get even with you, and the only thing that'll get me even is killing you. You're as good as dead right now. Don't make no mistake about that!"

Chapter 9

"I don't guess it ever crossed your mind it might be *you* that's making the mistake," Longarm replied mildly. "You don't even know yet what all you're up against. You and Annie and this fellow's just small fry compared to the folks you're trying to buck."

Stepping up to Longarm, the Apache Kid slapped the lawman's face twice, swinging his hand back and forth. Then, in a voice tinged with sullenness, he said, "Keep outa this, Long! Even if you don't know it, you're a dead man right this minute!"

Raising his hand again, the Kid once more started to strike Longarm, but Dorsey caught his wrist and stopped it in mid-air.

"Now, hold up, Kid!" he commanded. "I ain't on Longarm's side, but what he just said made sense."

"Not to me it didn't!" the Kid replied. There was a sneer in his voice as he went on, "This is my territory out here on Frenchman Flat, Dorsey. I don't need a bunch of city dudes to give me orders!"

"You're glad enough to take their money, I notice," Dorsey retorted. "Now, let's quit fighting about who's going to run this job. All of us are working for the same boss, and we know what he's like. He don't pay anybody that won't do what he tells 'em to, and that goes for you and Annie, Kid."

"Are you trying to tell us he's changed his mind about me and my boy working on this job?" she asked, frowning.

"That ain't what I said at all, Annie," Dorsey replied. "What I'm getting at is that I come here to see that everything goes the way the boss wants it to."

"That sounds to me like you're going to push me and my boy outside," Annie prodded.

"Not for a minute," Dorsey protested. "The boss has got a few things he wants done a certain way, that's all."

"Let's hear what they are," the Apache Kid put in. "Seeing that the boss has sent you out here to tell us what we're supposed to do."

"You'll hear soon enough," Dorsey promised. "Except there's something I got to do first. I ain't had time to tell you this yet, but there's two more fellows with me, and they talked to the boss just like I did before we started."

"Why didn't you tell me there was some more men with you?" the Kid demanded. "Where the hell are they?"

"They're waiting outside," Dorsey replied. "I aim to go after 'em right now. We'll all talk about what's the best way to handle Long, and then we'll do whatever the most of us decides is best."

"Why didn't they come in here with you?" Annie asked.

"Because we didn't know what to figure on. We come across what we taken to be a stray horse while we was on the way here," Dorsey explained. "We didn't see no signs around of anybody it belonged to, but the nag gave me the idea that you and Annie might be in some kind of trouble. I left the others outside to keep their eyes peeled, just in case whoever the horse belonged to might be on the prowl outside your cave."

"Which he wasn't," Annie broke in quickly. "But even if you hadn't come along, we wouldn't've been in any kind of bind."

"No, but you wasn't far from being. Long was getting ready to make his move on you and your boy when I shoved my gun into his ribs," Dorsey reminded her.

"If he'd tried anything, me and the Kid would've took care of him," Annie retorted.

"Maybe. But if you hadn't of, and Longarm had got away, all of us would be in trouble," Dorsey pointed out.

"So you say," the Kid broke in. "Like Annie said, we'd've handled him by ourselves if you hadn't happened to come along when you did."

"That's as may be," Dorsey replied placatingly. "Anyways, I left them other fellows outside because after we picked up Longarm's horse, I had a hunch somebody that didn't have no business being here might still be sneaking around. I figured if there was, we'd have a chance to get him sandwiched in between us, which is just how it worked out. And you got to admit, it was me that stopped Longarm from getting the jump on you."

Longarm had been listening with growing hope that the argument between the trio might open a way to let him break free. He tried to fan the dispute into open antagonism.

Now he commented, "You're smarter'n I taken you to be, Dorsey. If you're just smart enough—"

"Shut up, Long!" Dorsey snapped. "Or I'll stuff a gag in that flapping mouth of yours!"

"Suppose you just go back to telling us about them two men you got waiting outside," the Apache Kid broke in. "Who the hell are they, and why'd you bring 'em?"

"I brought 'em along because the boss told me to," Dorsey replied. "That was a good enough reason for me, so I guess it's good enough for you. And soon as I get 'em in here, you'll find out why."

"Go get 'em, then," Apache Annie said. "I'd sorta like to know why they're here myself."

"Sure," Dorsey nodded. "And while I go out to fetch 'em, you and the Kid can get Longarm trussed up nice and tight so he won't give us any more trouble."

"Don't worry, we'll take care of him," Annie promised. As Dorsey started out of the cavern, she turned to the Kid and went on, "There's a bunch of rawhide straps in that bundle over there that we can use. Bring 'em over by the fire so we can see what we're doing."

"Damn it, we're just wasting time," the Kid grumbled as he started toward the scattered packages that lay by the wall of the cavern. "Why don't we just shoot the son of a bitch right now and get it over with?"

"Because he might be able to tell us something it'd be handy to know about," Annie retorted as she prodded Longarm toward the fire with the barrel of her rifle. She said to him, "Go on. Step along peaceful, now. Don't make any more trouble for us, or I might start slicing you up by myself right this minute."

"Like hell you will!" the Apache Kid told her over his shoulder as he rummaged among the bundles. "Longarm's mine, Ma. Maybe if you feel like helping me work on him—"

"You're getting too big for your britches," Annie snapped. "You left our people too soon for me to finish teaching you to act like an Apache ougl.t to."

"Don't worry," the Kid told her as he came up carrying a handful of thin leather thongs. "I learned enough while I was in the pen to make up for what you didn't have time to show me."

"If it was left up to me, I could get along without either one of you," Longarm remarked. He realized the risk he was running by interfering in their argument, but still he had a faint hope that somehow he could turn their quarrel to his own advantage. "Now, you ain't gone too far with them fellows outside to be in a lot of real trouble yet, but if you go on messing around with the railroad—"

"Shut up!" the Apache Kid snapped. He grabbed Longarm's wrists and pulled them together, wrapped one of the thongs around them, and tossed the remaining leather strips to Annie. "I got his wrists tight," he told her. "You take care of his arms while I tie off the knots."

"I see you didn't forget the way to tie somebody up while you was in the pen," Apache Annie remarked as she stepped behind Longarm.

She pushed a thong between his side and his elbow, ran it around his back, and looped it through his arm and chest on the other side of his body. Then she began tightening the stout leather strap to pull his elbows together. While Annie worked, the Kid had knotted the thong that held Longarm's wrists in front of his chest. The pressure of the loop passed through his bent arms forced Longarm to raise his bound hands as he tried to ease the cutting pressure of the narrow leather straps.

Annie planted a knee in the small of Longarm's back and pulled on the thong that was looped through his bent elbows until its tension forced his shoulders up and back as his forearms were drawn still more tightly against his chest. He felt Annie's fingers brush against his upper arms as she tied the thong.

Now the Apache Kid dropped to one knee and started looping another of the straps around Longarm's ankles. Annie pushed her son's hands away before he could secure the first knot.

"Leave his legs for now," she said. "He can't get out of the cave with us and the others around, and we'll be taking him someplace else to get rid of him."

"I hadn't thought about that," the Kid said, standing up.

"So I noticed," Annie told him tartly. "Like I said, you still got a lot to learn, so don't—"

Whatever she might have intended to say was lost as Dorsey returned with the two men who'd been watching outside the cave.

"This is Haven and the other one's Sadler," he said, nodding in turn at the two men with him.

Both were rough-looking characters. On one cheek Haven had the scab of a healing wound that appeared to be a knife-slash. He carried a Maynard long-range target rifle in one hand and full bandolier of cartridges was draped around one shoulder. Sadler's gunbelt supported a pair of ivory-handled Smith and Wesson Russian Model .44's and Longarm noted in a quick professional survey that the deeply checkered grips were worn almost smooth. Both men had the aggressive jaw-set and cold eyes of gunhands.

Dorsey told his companions, "I've already told you men about Apache Annie and her kid. Now, let's all set down and go over what we got to do."

"What about him?" the man named Haven asked, pointing to Longarm. "Ain't he the federal marshal you was talking about?"

"Sure, but you can see for yourselves that he's not going to give us any trouble," Dorsey answered. "We'll get rid of him before we start our job."

"He'll be listening to every damn word that every one of us says," Haven pointed out. "Maybe we better put him outa the way first and talk after we're shut of him."

"Don't worry," Dorsey replied. "He'll never get a chance to tell anybody what we talk about. As soon as I get through laying things out, we'll take him out and get rid of him."

"Like hell we will!" the Apache Kid snapped. "Longarm's mine. He's gonna hurt a lot before he dies."

"Wait a minute!" Sadler broke in. "You mean that fellow tied up over there's the federal marshal they call Longarm?"

"That's right," the Kid nodded. "And I got a special score to settle with him."

"Now, I might have something to say about that," Longarm observed. His voice was as calm as though he was speaking to the others across a dinner table. "First off, I don't think a one of you knows how much you're biting off when you go up against the bunch that's out to build this railroad."

"What d'you mean by that?" Sadler asked before Dorsey could speak again.

"Why, it ain't just me you're going against, or a little bunch of men out marking right-of-way," Longarm replied quickly. He turned his head to look at Dorsey and went on, "Didn't you tell these poor fellows who they'll be bucking out here?"

"Shut up, Long!" Dorsey snapped. "Or I'll stop your mouth with a gag!"

"Not before I tell your friends they'll be going up against Barton Calder and me both if they lay a hand on anybody that's working on the railroad survey," Longarm said quickly.

He smiled inwardly when his mention of Calder's name brought an immediate reaction.

"You didn't say nothing to me about Bart Calder when I hired on this job," Haven protested, turning to Dorsey.

"You didn't tell me you were all that particular who you hired your gun to," Dorsey retorted.

"I don't recall Longarm's name coming up, either," Sadler put in. "And from what I heard about him, it don't much matter how tight he's tied up or what kind of a hole you put him in, he's going to snake out of it. Hell, Dorsey, anybody west of the Kansas City stockyards ought've told you that!"

"Be sensible, now!" Dorsey protested. "All you got to do is look at the way he's harnessed up. You can see he's not in shape to give us any kind of trouble!"

"Just the same—" Sadler began.

Dorsey cut him short. "Now, you quit flapping that big mouth of yours, Sadler! And you keep quiet, too, Haven."

"You're the one that's been doing most of the talking, Dorsey," Apache Annie broke in. "And we sure ain't going to get nowhere if we keep flap-jawing this way. The trouble is that all of us is tired and needs to rest a while."

"That's the first sensible word I've heard since we got here," Haven observed. "All of us is edgy. Me and Sadler and Dorsey's just put a lot of miles back of us, and we're acting like it. I don't know about the rest of you, but I'm so hungry my belly thinks my throat's been cut. I say we do like Annie said, and rest a while before we try to talk any more."

"I'll go you one better," Annie added quickly. "I say that after we've ate and you men get a little shut-eye, you three go with the Kid and let him show you what me and him has already figured out to do."

"Hell, I know what we've come here to do, Annie!" Dorsey protested. "Besides, on the way here me and Sadler and Haven's looked at about all of Nevada we're interested in seeing."

"If we're gonna sharpshoot that railroad survey gang the way you said, it'll be a big help to know the way the land lays," Haven said.

"He's right, Dorsey," Sadler agreed. "I feel the same way."

"It ain't a long ways to ride if you angle cross-country," the Apache Kid put in. "And by the time we'd start out your horses will be rested. Then when we come back here, we can do whatever palavering we need to before we start the job."

"I say Annie and the Kid makes sense, Dorsey," Haven urged. "I'd a sight rather know what I'm getting into than to go into strange country and have to learn how the land lays before I start work."

"That goes for me, too," Sadler said quickly.

"All right, then," Dorsey agreed. "We'll do it your way this time, but don't get any idea that I'm going to give up on calling the shots for you men. And that goes for you and your boy, too, Annie. Now, let's get our bedrolls in here if we're going to sleep a while. This floor looks pretty hard to me."

"Bring your horses in," Annie told the trio as they stood up and started toward the mouth of the cavern. "Kid, you go with them and bring Long's horse in, too. There ain't much chance of anybody passing by and seeing 'em during the night, but I don't believe in taking any chances."

When the dispute between the hired killers had started to develop, Longarm saw the chance of an opportunity to break free. For an instant he'd been tempted to speak up in support of Haven and Sadler, but a moment of thought was all he needed to set aside that impulse. Now, as the three hired killers started out of the cavern, he welcomed in silence the decision they'd made to delay starting their foray against the survey party and set his mind to work trying to think of a way he might use their absence to his advantage.

Annie paid no attention to him while she moved around clearing the floor to make room for the men's bedrolls. Longarm racked his brain vainly for an idea, something on which he could hang a plan for action, but he'd still gotten nowhere when Dorsey and the others returned.

There was a brief period of bustling around while Dorsey and his men spread their bedrolls and got settled for the night. The Apache Kid picked up the lantern as Annie moved to the side of the cavern opposite the newcomers and began kicking at the two scrambled heaps of bedding that lay along the wall.

Longarm had watched the activities of the group in silence, deciding that the least attention he drew to himself the better, but when he saw the Kid pick up the lantern he realized that unless he made some kind of protest he would be spending a very uncomfortable night sitting in the middle of the hard floor.

"Ain't you going to spread my bedroll for me?" he asked.

"I don't see why I should," the Apache Kid replied. "I didn't get any more care while I was in that prison you sent me to than you're likely to get."

"Damn it, I wasn't running the prison!" Longarm protested. "And I didn't pull off the job you got sent up for, either!"

Unexpectedly, Annie spoke up from her position beside the wall where she was straightening out two sets of bedding. "Go on and fix his blankets," she told her son. "Put him over there, between us and Dorsey's outfit, so he'll have to pass by both of us if he tries to get away during the night."

Moving with slow reluctance, the Apache Kid untied the strings that held Longarm's blanket roll to the saddle-shirt and tossed the bedding against the wall in a rumpled heap.

"There's your bed," he said, starting toward his own blankets. "But damned if I'll help you to it. Get there by yourself any way you can."

Longarm had no intention of starting an argument with the Kid or anybody else. He'd realized that the less attention he drew to himself, the better his lot would be, and the better his chances of being ignored while he tried to figure out a way to escape. He began dragging himself across the bumpy floor with the heels of his boots.

He could advance only a few inches at a time, and long before he reached his bedroll the Kid had blown out the lantern. Longarm continued his slow progress in the dark, and when he reached the crumpled heap of blankets he had no way to spread them. At last he kicked and toed them into a crude rectangle and rolled over on them.

At first the blankets seemed soft and restful, but before he'd lain on them very long he began to become aware of bumps and humps jabbing into him from the granules of gypsum that protruded from the floor. Long ago he had lost all the feeling in his hands, and when he tried to flex his fingers he discovered that he was unable to tell whether or not they were moving.

By dint of much wriggling and bootsole-scuffling, Longarm managed to push himself to the wall of the cavern. After a few minutes spent in maneuvering, he squirmed and got his boot soles braced solidly enough on the floor so that he could maneuver to bring his back and shoulders up and sit erect, his knees bent up in front of him, his back against the wall.

Snores were sounding now from the sleeping gunmen, and now and then one of the horses in the outer cavern let out a soft, breathy whuffle. Staring into the pitchy blackness, seeing nothing, Longarm shook his head slowly.

Old son, he mused, *you ain't been in this bad of a pickle for quite a while. And you better figure a way to get out of it right soon, or you'll learn what it feels like to be dead.*

Somehow, the grisly thought failed to stimulate his thinking. After spending what seemed to be a very long time in futile consideration of plans that he quickly realized had no chance of working, Longarm's head fell forward and within a few moments he went to sleep.

Chapter 10

Longarm awoke from an uncomfortable sleep, his mind alert as his eyes snapped open. He knew he'd been awakened by a noise, but he was uncertain of its source. Darkness still hung pitch-black and veiled the cave. The dull, staccato thunking of horses' hooves on the floor broke the silence and Longarm relaxed, realizing at once what had broken his sleep.

Even though he hadn't been able to stretch and relax, the night's fitful dozing had rested him. He struggled into a half-sitting, half-lying position, leaning against the wall, and realized as he moved that his arms and hands were even more useless than they had been the night before.

He was trying to flex his fingers, with very little success, when the harsh sound of a phosphor match being scratched across metal sounded above the dying noise of the hoofbeats. The flame that flickered into life as the match touched the lantern's wick seemed as bright to him as sunshine at high noon. Suddenly his eyes began watering. He blinked to clear them, and the lantern light no longer seemed sun-bright, but it was still bright enough to be uncomfortable.

Longarm slitted his lids and in a moment or two his eyes had gotten used to the light. He saw Apache Annie standing beside her bedroll, holding the lantern. Its wick was still flickering, but soon it settled down to shed a steady glow. She had apparently gone to bed fully clothed, for she looked just as she had the night before. Glancing at the bedroll that had been occupied by the Apache Kid, he saw that it was empty, the blankets tossed aside in disarray.

Sounds of muffled stirring began coming from the killers' bedrolls as Annie's moccasin-clad feet scuffled across the hard floor. She slowed her shuffling pace when she reached Longarm, and stopped to look at him. He stared up into her obsidian eyes but said nothing. After she had gazed at him for a moment, she grunted and moved on to the bedrolls where the gunmen were beginning to sit up, yawning, rubbing their eyes, and stretching.

"Damn it, Annie, why'd you wake us up?" Dorsey complained, "The way it looks, it's still the middle of the night."

"Daytime soon," she replied. "Boy's taking horses to drink. Outside's cool now, you can ride fast. Move slow while you look at railroad camp. Wait till near dark before you start back, so it cool for horses."

"She makes pretty good sense, Dorsey," Haven commented as he sat up in his bedding and started levering his feet into his boots. "It was so hot in the middle of the day yesterday while we was riding here that all our nags was damn near blowed before we got halfway across Frenchman Flat. So was we, if you come right down to it."

"I guess," Dorsey grunted. "But I could sure do with an hour or two more shut eye."

"You ain't no sleepier'n me," Sadler put in.

Dorsey looked up from the gunbelt he was buckling on. "The quicker we get through with this job, the sooner we'll draw down the rest of what's coming to us," he pointed out. His voice had lost its waking-up laziness. "And we damn sure won't get much done if we lallygag around. Now, soon as I get outside and do my business, I'll be ready to ride. If you fellows wanta go, you better be ready, too."

"Don't we get no breakfast?" Haven asked.

"Whatever's left in our saddlebags will carry us till we get back. We'll eat while we're riding," Dorsey replied. He turned to face Apache Annie once more. "You have us some grub ready when we get back, Annie."

"You got food to fix? Boy and me are run short," she told the outlaw.

"Don't worry. I dropped a towsack up by where we hitched the horses last night. It's got some airtights in it, and spuds and stuff. I figured you'd need 'em before we're finished."

Annie nodded and turned away. After the three gunmen had led their horses out of the cave and the noise of their departing hoofbeats had died away, she came back to stand and look down at Longarm.

"I guess maybe you're hungry," she said.

Her voice was flat and devoid of any feeling, but just as Mururi's English had shown a swift improvement when the occasion demanded it, Annie no longer seemed reluctant to talk in something other than the half-pidgin tongue she had used while the outlaws were in the cave.

Longarm could not tell from her words whether she was promising breakfast or just prodding his feelings to make him feel worse. Even though his stomach had been sending him urgent messages since he woke up, he had no intention to beg.

"Well, I ain't going to say I'd turn down a bite," he told her. "But I can get along for a spell without eating yet."

"I'll make some fire. My breakfast time, too."

"I tell you what I'd as soon have as breakfast," Longarm said, deciding that he had nothing to lose by trying. "I got some cigars in my vest pocket here, if you and that boy of yours didn't bust 'em all up when you tied me last night. Now, I'd take it as a real favor if you'd let me have a hand free so's I can light up a smoke."

Annie did not answer for a moment, but stood looking down at Longarm. He watched her, his face as expressionless as hers, while she looked at the leather thongs that held his wrists jutting out from his chest and pulled his elbows together behind his back. He had almost given up hope of getting a reply when she nodded.

"All right," she agreed.

Groping in the folds of her flowing skirt, Annie produced a nickel-plated pistol. Longarm recognized it at a glance as a Colt .41 National Derringer. The once-bright coating on the gun's oddly shaped, squared barrel showed pits and tarnish, but Longarm had no doubt that the stubby little pistol was in good working order and that Annie would have no hesitation about using it.

She tucked the derringer into her left armpit, where it was almost out of sight, and held her upper arm close to her side as she bent over Longarm. With one hand she grabbed the thongs that crossed in front of his chest and pulled him upright against the wall. Then she loosened the thongs around his wrists and watched while he rubbed his hands together and flexed his fingers until he could move them freely again.

"That's as far as I'm going to untie you," Annie told Longarm after his hand was freed. She stood watching him flex his fingers as he tried to bring feeling back into his hand. "And soon as you smoke your cigar I'll tie your arm tight again. One damn sure thing, you ain't going to catch me leaving you loose any time I got to turn my back to you."

"Wait a minute, now! I never backshot nobody in my life!" Longarm protested.

"I never said you did. But I've heard plenty about how fast you are on the draw."

"Ain't you forgetting that Dorsey took away my Colt?"

"Now, he did, for a fact," Annie nodded. Reaching into her armpit, she produced the derringer again. "Just the same, I'll tie you up again soon as you light your cigar. Go on, now, light up, so I can start fixing breakfast."

"Have it your way," Longarm shrugged.

He pulled out one of his long, slender cigars. The wrapper was not cracked, but the slim brown cylinder had taken on a small curve. Longarm bent his head and found that with a little stretching he could get the cigar in his mouth. He struck a match on his thumbnail and puffed the cigar until it was drawing well. Annie had watched his every move closely, and he had had no opportunity to palm his derringer while his hand was free. He gripped the cigar in his teeth and let his arm dangle down while he flexed his fingers.

"That's plenty to get you limbered up," Annie said sharply. "Turn around now, so I can tie you up again."

Longarm had known Annie would re-tie his arm, but he had counted on the rope leaving him a bit more slack than he'd had before. He was quickly disappointed. She was careful to keep her derringer away from him, where he could not reach it as she pulled the rope tight. When Longarm tried covertly to move his partly freed forearm, he found that he had very little more movement in it than he'd had earlier, and the knot was as firm as the first one had been.

Stepping back when she had pulled the double-looped knot tight, Annie nodded with satisfaction and said, "That oughta hold you just as good as before. Now go on and finish your cigar while I scrape up something for us to eat."

Longarm puffed on the cigar while Annie got fresh lumps of charcoal from the gunnysack by the wall and strewed it over the night-dead coals in the pan she used as a brazier. She took a spouted tin can from behind the sack of charcoal and squirted a colorless liquid over the charcoal in the brazier, then extracted a match from a pocket of her shapeless dress and lighted the oil.

Blue flames danced for a moment, but flickered out when she leaned forward to blow on the brazier. Soon her swarthy face was reflecting a red glow. Annie lifted a coffeepot from the floor and set it on the coals.

"Last night's," she said to Longarm as she started toward the entrance to the cavern. "Takes too long to make a fresh pot, and there's enough in here to go with breakfast. After a while I'll brew up some more."

Annie disappeared behind the entry wall for several minutes. When she returned she was carrying a bulging flour sack. Untying the knot that held the sack closed, she inspected its contents, then turned to Longarm again.

"Dorsey done pretty good," she told Longarm. "There's fresh bakery bread and tomatoes and peaches in airtights and a lot of fresh potatoes. I ain't had peaches for quite a spell. They oughta go down pretty good for breakfast."

Annie went to the wall where she and the Kid had bunked down and rummaged behind the bedding for a moment. Longarm's eyes widened a bit when he saw what she held in her hand when she straightened up. It was an Indian war hatchet, its long narrow blade an arc that curved gently down to a sharp cutting edge on one end, the other end tapered to a long spiked tip.

Longarm looked at it in surprise. Apaches had for the most part abandoned the use of such weapons a hundred years earlier, when traders began supplying them with guns. He said nothing, however. Annie picked up a cloth-swathed bundle in her free hand and returned to the grill. A thread of steam was beginning to rise from the coffeepot. She put the hatchet and her bundle on the floor and hunkered down beside the grill.

"I got some cheese left from what me and the boy been eating on," she said. "We'll have a hunk of it with this bakery bread and some peaches. Don't that strike you as a pretty good breakfast?"

Before Longarm could answer she picked up the can of peaches and began hacking an X-shaped cut in the top, using the war hatchet. She pried the triangular sections of tin upward, fished out a piece of peach, and popped it into her mouth.

After she'd chewed and swallowed, she went on, "Not that I give a damn what you like or don't like. You can eat what I do or leave it alone."

"Whatever suits you suits me, I guess," Longarm said. He spoke around the cigar. Its stub was still clamped in his mouth, and he reached up with his free hand to remove it, but the rope that bound his elbows was too tight. His fingers fell just short of his chin.

Dropping his hand, he puffed the cigar stud until it began to burn his lips, then spat it out. He said, "You can't start feeding me too soon, Annie. But how in tunket do you figure I'm going to eat unless you undo my hands?"

Annie had popped another wedge of peach into her mouth and was chewing it. "You still got one hand loose. Use it," she said.

"If you was looking, you just seen me try to get my cigar outa my mouth," Longarm told her. "I can't reach it, tied up by my elbows the way I am."

"Looks like I'll just have to feed you," she said. "I damn sure ain't going to let you get both your hands loose."

"Whenever you get around to it, then," he said.

"I guess I'll have to drag you over here while you eat," Annie frowned. "Damned if I'm going to run over there to you every time you want a bite."

"All you got to do is untie my legs," Longarm suggested. "I'd a sight rather walk than get dragged."

"I ain't soft in the head," she told him. She walked over to Longarm and stood looking down at him for a moment, then said, "Tighten your butt up and you'll slide right along. The floor ain't t all that rough."

Before Longarm could protest, Annie grabbed his ankles and began pulling him toward the center of the cave. Longarm braced himself and succeeded in keeping his balance as she dragged him across the bumpy floor. Luckily, the distance was short and he was still sitting upright when Annie dropped his booted feet and moved around the boxes within reach of the sack of food.

She dipped her fingers into the can of peaches and ate another piece. After she'd chewed and swallowed she looked at Longarm and asked, "You want some of these peaches now?"

"Not right this minute. I'd rather start with the bread and cheese."

Annie broke off a hunk of cheese and popped it into Longarm's mouth. She waited for him to chew it down a bit, then fed him piece of bread. She went back to eating from the can of peaches while she watched Longarm chewing.

After she'd downed another piece of the syrup-drenched fruit, she moved wordlessly to the fire, filled a tin cup with coffee, and put it on the floor beside him. Longarm picked up the cup, but he could not bring it to his lips. He looked at Annie and shook his head.

"There ain't no way I can drink that coffee if you don't loosen up on my hands," he told her.

"Well, I ain't untying you," she said quickly. "But I'll hold the cup for you if you're ready for coffee. Or do you want to eat some more, first?"

"Another bite of bread and cheese'd sure go down real good," he nodded.

Annie fed him the bread and cheese, then gave her attention to the peaches again. After Longarm had chewed and swallowed once more, he told her, "If you'll fish me a piece of peach outa that can, and hold that coffee cup so's I can drink some of it, I'll call it a breakfast."

"There's just enough peaches left for you and me both to have another piece," she said, fishing around in the can. She found a section of peach and shoved it into Longarm's mouth, took out another piece for herself and ate it, then tilted the can to her lips and drained the remaining syrupy juice into her mouth. "Now that makes me feel a lot better," she went on. "If you had enough breakfast, I guess you want some more coffee now?"

"I guess," Longarm nodded.

He'd been watching Annie covertly while they ate, puzzled by the sudden change in her attitude toward him. She moved closer to him and picked up the coffee cup. Kneeling beside him, she held it to his mouth while he drank. When she set the cup down she leaned back on her heels and gazed at him silently.

After a moment Longarm said to Annie, "Not that it's any of my business, but it seems like you're being a lot nicer to me today than you was last night. Mind telling me why?"

Her face expressionless, she said, "Well, maybe it's on account of I don't have to worry about you jumping me and getting away, as long as I keep you tied up."

Still puzzled, Longarm decided he would get no information from Annie without questioning her. He asked, "Have I got something wrong with me, Annie? I noticed you been looking at me sorta funny for a long time."

"I guess I have, but I didn't know I was showing it," she replied. "You know, I been out here with nobody but my boy for quite a spell, Longarm. I figured when Dorsey and his men got here one of them could give me what I need, but it didn't work out that way. By now, I don't feel like waiting no longer. I need a man real bad, and it's going to be you, whether you like it or not."

Although other women had said much the same thing to Longarm at one time or another, they had usually been a little less forthright and the surroundings had been different. He gazed at Annie with open astonishment. Her obsidian eyes did not blink, and her face showed no emotion.

"I guess you mean what I think you mean," he frowned.

"I sure do. And I don't feel like waiting any longer."

Annie kneeled beside Longarm as she spoke. Her fingers went to his belt buckle, and after she had loosened it she turned her attention to the buttons on his trousers. Her moves were so swift that Longarm had no time to protest before she had begun pulling his pants down to his thighs.

"Damn it, Annie!" he exclaimed. "Don't I have nothing to say about this?"

"No. So don't waste your breath," she replied.

Longarm realized that he could do nothing to stop Annie from doing anything she wanted to. He kept quiet and lay motionless while her callused fingers caressed him and made no effort to move even after she released him and rose to her knees. She tugged at her full-cut skirt until she could bunch it around her waist. He lay helpless while Annie continued her attentions, then lifted her hips and sank down on his rigid shaft until she'd engulfed him fully. She sighed deeply as she began rocking to and fro, her weight keeping Longarm pinned down to the floor.

Longarm lay motionless, his eyes fixed on Annie's broad face hovering above him as she swayed back and forth. She was smiling now, a wide grin that exposed her strong yellowed teeth between her broad taut lips. She kept her hips in constant motion, jerking them back and forth in a rhythm that grew faster and faster as the minutes ticked away.

In spite of himself, Longarm was responding, but he was far from peaking when Annie began sighing in time with her body's rhythmic gyrations. Her sighs grew in intensity and the tempo of her swaying increased as the seconds ticked away. After a short while the speed of her gyrations increased and her sighs turned into small cries. The cries increased in volume and soon one gasped, gusty exhalation followed another.

Annie's head tilted back, her face hidden from Longarm

now, but he did not need to see her to realize that she was reaching her peak. There was nothing that he could do by now, but he'd resolved from the outset that he'd show no pleasure, no matter what he felt. He lay motionless while Annie swayed and writhed above him as her body trembled and her frantic wriggling peaked and passed. At last her quivers subsided. She opened her eyes and looked down at Longarm.

"Now that done me more good than a little bit!" she sighed. "And seeing as you didn't let go, I don't guess you'd mind if I start all over and do it again!"

Chapter 11

"It's sure too bad you ain't an Apache, Longarm," Annie sighed as she sat on her bedroll and propped herself up on her elbow to look across the cave at him. After she'd finally ended her lengthy session with Longarm she'd walked over to her bedroll and dropped onto its blankets. "Or at least a half-Apache like me."

"I take it you mean that complimentary-like," Longarm told her. "I ain't so sure I do. But I always figured your boy was a full-blood, the way he acted and all."

Annie stifled a yawn before going on. "The Kid's daddy was a full-blood," she said. "I ain't seen him for a long time, though. The last I heard, he was down on the Mexican border with Geronimo, fighting against General Miles. I guess if you hadn't arrested the Kid and got him sent to prison we'd both be down there, too."

"You stayed here and waited for the Kid to serve his time?"

"He didn't get but two years. And he's the only boy I got. Who'd've looked after him if I didn't?"

"Seems to me like he's old enough to look after himself now. He got into enough trouble before I run him down and taken him in for that job he pulled. And there ain't no better place to take on a load of meaness than the Territorial Prison. I know that for a fact."

He decided that he would say nothing to her about the part that the Apache Kid had played in leading him to the cave. That could wait until he'd managed to get his handcuffs on the Kid, though he admitted to himself that how and when he was going to be able to do that formed a big question mark. The important thing was to stop the killers from doing their work and wiping out the railroad survey party.

"I reckon you done your best with the Kid," he went on, "but you and him is both mixed up with real bad company now."

"That's about the only kind that'd have much to do with me," Annie replied. "Anyhow, I'm used to being in bad company by now, and it don't bother me none. Don't go feeling sorry for me, Longarm. Just shut up and let me rest. You better get some rest, too, because I aim to have another go with you before the Kid brings Dorsey and the others back here."

"Seems to me I oughta have something to say about that."

"Well, you don't, any more than I did when I was about ten years old and the Indian agent up at the Duck Creek reservation made a woman outa me."

"And you haven't had any use for white men since?"

"Hell, there ain't no difference between a white man and an Indian, Longarm." Annie snorted. "I oughta know."

Longarm decided the time had come to ask the question he had been holding in his mind since the trio of killers had arrived from the northern part of Nevada.

"I guess that goes for the man you're working for now?" he asked. "Or does he have something special you can't say no to?"

"Who said I was working for anybody?" Annie demanded.

"Nobody. But them three fellows that's out scouting with your boy right now is a dead giveaway, you oughta know that.

106

I bet a double eagle to a rotten apple that they're getting paid by the same man you are."

"That's just your guess," Annie retorted. "Now, stop flapping your jaws and let me go back to sleep for an hour or so."

Longarm fell silent and bided his time. He was rewarded in a very short time when Annie's eyes closed and her breathing settled into the slow rhythm that told him she was asleep.

As soon as he was sure Annie was sleeping deeply, Longarm began carrying out the plan that had sprung almost full-blown into his mind as he watched Annie start toward her bedding. The tomahawk she had used to open the can of peaches lay only a few feet away. Moving as silently as his bonds would allow him to, Longarm rolled toward it. By arcing his back and pushing his slick boot soles as hard as he dared on the floor, he inched along until he could close his left hand over its handle.

For what seemed to him an interminable time, the head-heavy tomahawk defeated Longarm's efforts as he tried with his partly free left hand to place its edge in the exact spot that would sever the thong holding his right arm and hand immobile. Finally he managed to guide the blade to its mark. A few quick touches of the razor-sharp edge against the thongs parted the taut strip of leather. With his right hand free, Longarm made quick work of severing the remaining ties.

For a minute or two he sat motionless, waiting for feeling to return to his cramped limbs. When they returned to normal, he slid his derringer from his vest pocket and stepped silently to the pallet where Annie still lay sleeping. He pressed the muzzle of his derringer to Annie's forehead and her eyes popped open.

"Just don't move a smidgen," Longarm told her. "I hate to shoot a woman, but I sure won't let my feelings stop me from putting a bullet in *your* brain, Annie."

"Don't worry," she replied. "I know by now when a man means what he says. I guess you'll want my gun. You know where it is."

Longarm took the Colt National derringer from the capacious pocket of Annie's skirt and slid it into his pocket.

"Looks like it's your turn to get tied up," he said. "I don't aim to have you getting in my way when them killer friends of yours gets back. I figure I got about an hour to get ready to surprise 'em."

"I don't give a damn about Dorsey and his bunch," Annie told him. "But don't shoot my boy, Longarm. He's about all I got left in the world."

"I can't make you no promise like that, Annie," Longarm replied. "You oughta know better'n to ask. But if you was to tell me who you're working for, and then help me corral them fellows that's with the Kid, it's likely I can take 'em without having to do a lot of shooting."

"Hell, I heard that too many times before," Annie said. "I can't go against my own flesh and blood! I'm sorry, but that's the way it is."

"Sorry's got nothing to do with it," Longarm said quickly. "If Dorsey and his killers ain't stopped, they're gonna stir up enough of a ruckus to start Bart Calder sending telegrams to Washington. First thing you know, he'll have the army sending a bunch of troops down here to run things. They won't fool around with Dorsey and his crew, which takes in you and the Kid."

"I don't give a damn what happens to Dorsey's outfit," Annie said. "All I care about is me and the boy. If I tell you, will you promise to go easy on my son?"

"That's a promise I can't make, and I guess you know it," Longarm said slowly. "At least, not till I know a whole lot more about who you and him's working for. But I'll make you this much of a promise right here and now: If there's shooting, and your boy's mixed up in it, I'll do my best not to kill him."

"Which means you'll do your best to kill him if I *don't* tell you!" she snapped.

"I didn't say that, and I didn't mean it," Longarm said. "If it comes to a showdown fight, there ain't much I can do to keep him from getting killed. But if you tell me what I want to know, chances are there won't *be* no fighting showdown."

Annie was silent for a long moment. Then she said, "You was talking about Bart Calder a while back. I guess you know there's folks here in Nevada that don't hold with his ways and what he's doing."

"I don't suppose he's any different from anybody else that's made a lot of money and is out to make a lot more," Longarm said thoughtfully. "But even if Calder was the one that got me sent out here from Denver, I ain't working for him. I'm just trying to keep things peaceful."

"I don't guess I thought about it that way before," Annie frowned. She was silent for a moment, then went on, "I ain't going to give you no names, Longarm. But there's a bunch of men up in Silver City that'd taken over a gold strike from a prospector over to the southeast of Frenchman Flat. They don't want no railroad poking its tracks down here."

"Are you sure about that, Annie?" Longarm frowned. "It'd seem to me they'd *want* a railroad, to haul their ore out."

Annie shook her head. "Not this bunch. They aim to build a stamping mill and all the rest of it and hire Indians to work 'em. They figure they'll make more because they won't have to pay the Ho people as much as they would their own kind."

"And Calder's messing up their plans by getting a railroad started down here, is that right?"

"Just about. Even if his railroad ain't going where they'd like to put one in later on, they ain't got no use for Bart Calder anyhow."

"So they hired you to come down here and—".

"Not me. My boy. Now you've showed up and, from what I've heard him say, you're likely to bust up their scheme. Now, I've told you all I know about it. You can just keep quiet, because I ain't going to listen to no more of your palaver."

Tied up as she was, turning away from Longarm was no easy job, but Annie managed to do it. Longarm paid no further attention to her. Standing in the middle of the cave, he began trying to work out a way to surprise the killers when they returned.

Two cups of coffee, a snack of cheese and bread, and a cigar later, Longarm was no closer to a plan than he had been when he was still lying tied and helpless on the cave floor. Annie had not moved. He could not tell by glancing at her whether she was awake or asleep, and whichever it was made no real difference as long as she refused to help him in catching the killer gang.

One thing you know for sure, old son, he told himself silently. *You better not fritter away no more time. Them fellers has been gone quite a spell, and if they come back and catch you inside this damn cave you'll be ten miles up shit creek without no paddle.*

Longarm glanced around the cave, saw nothing that would help him, and went to the jog that led to its mouth. The livery horse was still standing there, tethered to a short picket-line which he realized the murder gang must have set up to accommodate their own mounts. If Annie had a horse, it was nowhere in sight. Longarm walked around the rump of his own mount. It had not been unsaddled, his rifle was in the saddle-scabbard, and his saddlebags appeared untouched.

"Them damn killers was in too big of a hurry to do what any sensible man would've took care of first thing," he muttered. "Was I in their place, before I'd done anything else, I'd've unsaddled this horse and taken away that rifle."

He pulled the Winchester out of its scabbard and checked its magazine. The tube was full, a shell was in the chamber, and the rifle appeared to be untouched. Leaving nothing to chance, Longarm ejected the shell from the chamber and levered the next cartridge into it, then picked up the unfired round and put it back into the magazine. He replaced the rifle in its scabbard, untied the reins from the picket-line and led the horse outside.

A sort of semi-darkness still draped the land, but it was being dispelled by the first light of false dawn showing above the gully's eastern rim, draping the wide canyon itself in a crepuscular dimness that was neither light nor darkness but a deceptive mixture of both. The horse whinnied when the fresh morning air struck its nostrils. Longarm realized that the animal must have been standing at the picket-line for part of a day and a full night without water or fodder.

There was nothing he could do to feed it, but the spring

was not far away. He led the horse to the little pool formed by the trickle of water from the canyon wall and let it drink. The animal thrust its nose into the pool and whuffled as it began drinking. Longarm stepped up to the trickling spring that fed the pool and cupped his hand in the purling little stream to catch water, which he drank as thirstily as the horse.

After several gulps the horse raised its head, its ears twitching. Longarm watched the animal for a moment. The horse should still be drinking. Then the horse whinnied. It was not a loud-high-pitched, questioning whinny, but a short one of recognition, quickly smothered.

That was all the warning Longarm needed. Before letting the horse drink, he had folded the reins into a U and tucked the doubled leathers into the little open triangle formed by the arch of the McClellan saddle's hornless cantle. Now he caught the reins in a single sweeping grab and pulled the horse's head around. While it was still turning, he vaulted into the saddle and toed the animal back toward the mouth of the cave.

Almost as soon as he started moving, Longarm realized that the horse's warning had come just a few moments too late. He heard the muffled thunking of hoofbeats behind him and dug his heels into his mount's flanks. The horse quickened its pace, but Longarm had heard the muffled noises too late. Before he reached the point where a few more yards would have taken him out of sight of the approaching riders, he glanced behind him and saw Dorsey ride into view. Behind him Longarm got a glimpse of Haven and the Apache Kid. Sadler was nowhere in sight.

To get a better view of the canyon's widening floor, Dorsey was keeping his horse close to the sheer curving north wall. He and Longarm saw one another at almost the same instant. Longarm's years of almost constant battles against the lawless gave him the edge of a few seconds—an edge that had saved him many times in the past. Before Dorsey could bend forward and draw his rifle, Longarm had his hand around the stock of his Winchester.

Twisting in his saddle, Longarm snapshotted. The slug whistled home. Dorsey lurched backward with the impact of the hot lead as it tore into his chest. His extended arm dropped lifelessly away from his rifle-stock; then he crumpled slowly forward until his horse shied and dislodged his sagging body from the saddle to fall sprawled at the base of the canyon's wall and lie still in a motionless huddle.

Behind Dorsey's rearing horse the forms of the Apache Kid and Haven loomed in the steadily brightening light. Longarm was swinging the Winchester's muzzle toward the Kid when a blur of motion from Haven caught his eye. Changing his arm was a matter of habit formed of lessons learned in many shootouts.

Haven was shouldering his rifle when Longarm got him in the vee of the Winchester's sights and triggered off his second telling shot. Haven's rifle dropped to the canyon floor and kicked up a small puff of dusty sand as Longarm's whistling slug went home. The outlaw was knocked back in his saddle for a fraction of a second before he crumpled and began toppling.

The Apache Kid had been riding beside Haven. He sat his pony Indian-style, without stirrups or bit. His saddle was only a soft leather pad and instead of a bit his reins were attached to a narrow leather headstall that circled the horse's jaws.

Though Haven's tumbling form barely touched the Kid's horse, the shots and the blood-smell had spooked the animal. When the outlaw lurched sideways, falling from his saddle, he brushed against the Kid's already nervous mount. Before the Kid could react, the horse began whirling in a flash of stamping hooves. The Kid had nothing to grab and the leather loop lacked the firm control of a bit. Though he clung hard with his knees and thighs, the horse was already out of control before he began trying to curb it. The animal's wild dancing and rearing forced the Kid to grab the horse's mane to keep from being thrown.

He was carrying his rifle Apache-style, at a slant across his back, held there by a narrow sling of soft leather over one shoulder. With both hands locked in his horse's mane, the Apache Kid was as effectively out of action as though he had been totally unarmed.

Sadler came into sight just then. Unlike the Kid, he had his rifle in his hand. He brought it up before Longarm could shoulder his Winchester, but Longarm jerked his horse's reins and ducked forward as Sadler fired. The bullet whizzed angrily past Longarm, and by now the Kid had his horse under control. He, too, was leveling his rifle. Longarm saw his only chance and took it. He kicked his horse hard in its belly and the animal leaped across the canyon floor.

Sadler triggered off his shot a split-second too late. Though the rifle slug's breeze brushed Longarm's face, the lead was a quarter of an inch too wide. Before Sadler could lever a fresh round into his rifle's chamber, Longarm had reached the shelter that was provided by the curving wall of the canyon.

Now that he had started, Longarm kept moving. He heard the soft thunking of hoofbeats behind him and knew that his enemies were spurring after him. Hugging the curving canyon wall, he rode hell-for-leather toward the shelter of the cave, not really sure that he could reach it before the widening canyon floor robbed him of the dubious edge he had on his pursuers.

Sadler and the Kid came into sight just as Longarm glimpsed the mouth of the gypsum cave fifty yards ahead. The sudden daybreak of the high desert country was flooding the canyon brightly now. Longarm saw at once that to change his course and try to cross the widening canyon floor to reach the cave would be suicide.

He kicked his pony to a fresh burst of speed and the animal somehow found a reserve of strength that swept Longarm past the cave mouth and behind the curve in the canyon wall. Slugs from his pursuers rifles sang past and sent flakes of stone spurting from the side of the canyon beyond the curve. Longarm was in control of his half-spooked horse by now. He looked back and found that he could no longer see Sadler and the Apache Kid, though he could still hear their horses' hoofbeats thudding on the sandy floor.

Sadler came into view first, a few moments after Longarm had swept past the cave's mouth. Longarm had no time to shoulder his Winchester. Handling the rifle like a pistol, he brought up its barrel and let off a shot. The bullet hit the stock of the outlaw's rifle, the bullet's impact knocking the weapon out of Sadler's hands and sending it cartwheeling for several yards along the canyon floor.

By now the Apache Kid had come into sight. He had somehow managed to get his rifle-sling free and had the weapon in his hands. He saw Sadler's rifle fall, brought up his own weapon, and leveled it to get Longarm in his sights. Out of the long years of his experience Longarm had learned to count his shots. He knew that only one more round remained in the Winchester, and it was the round now in the chamber.

In his twisted-back position, forced to fire without the benefit of sighting, Longarm had only one choice. He let the muzzle of his Winchester drop to disable the Kid's horse and triggered off his last round before the Apache could fire. The Indian pony veered sharply and broke stride. Though it stayed on all four feet, its stumble spoiled the Kid's aim. The slug from his rifle went wild.

Sadler was still sitting his pony, drawing his pistol. The mouth of the gypsum cave yawned just across the canyon from the Kid. He yanked the reins of his stumbling mount and cut across the canyon toward the mouth of the gypsum cave, yelling to Sadler to follow him. His shout distracted Sadler as his trigger finger tightened. The slug from his pistol kicked up dust at the hooves of Longarm's horse.

When Sadler saw that he'd missed, he reined across the canyon to follow the Kid into the shelter of the cave. The echo of his last shot was still reverberating in the canyon when he vanished in the cavern's black yawning mouth.

Chapter 12

Longarm saw the outlaws disappear and reined his own mount across the canyon to get out of the line of fire from the cave. The echoes of Sadler's last shot had died away by now and the canyon was totally still. His hands moving with swift efficiency, he reloaded his Winchester. Longarm did not return the weapon to its saddle holster, but balanced it across the front of his saddle, while almost of their own volition the fingers of his free hand slid a cigar out of his vest pocket.

When he had flicked a match alight and puffed at the cigar until it was drawing satisfactorily, Longarm at last looked around to take stock of the section of the canyon to which the running gunfight had taken him.

This was his first view of the section of the big dry wash that lay beyond the mouth of the gypsum cave. Its walls did not curve here, but ran straight. Nor were they completely sheer and formed of unbroken talc-white rock; on the north side of the wide gully the wall was fractured and broken. Some great unheaval in the far-distant past had cracked the wall and pushed a huge section of it onto the floor of the canyon.

Over the ages the long, deep crevasse created by the fracture had been filled in as storms and whirling winds blew dust and debris from the canyon floor into it. The result of ages of such activity by the weather was the formation of a long ramplike shelf, wide enough to accommodate three or four horsemen abreast, or even a wagon.

This was the only spot Longarm had seen since entering the big gully that allowed passage from the floor of the dry wash to its rim. The thought of leaving the wash, where he had felt trapped, was a tempting one, but Longarm pushed it aside. The thought of Annie and the Kid and the surviving outlaw still holed up in the cave kept him from moving.

He glanced along the wall where he had sheltered, looking for signs of activity from the cave, but there were none. Shifting his gaze beyond the cave-mouth toward the spring, the sight of the two riderless horses and the sprawled bodies of Dorsey and Haven reminded him of the empty holster that dangled from his belt.

Old son, he told himself, *it ain't likely Dorsey'd let that Colt of yours get very far away from him. If you don't find it on his body, it'll be in his saddlebags for sure. None of them inside that cave is going to come out any time soon. They'll likely be too busy hashing over what's happened and what they can do next. If there ever was a time for you to go after your gun, right now is it.*

He nudged his horse with his booted toe and rode toward the dead outlaws. Before he'd covered the short distance to the cave's mouth, he reined in to listen. Voices were raised in angry argument inside. Apache Annie and her son were arguing with Sadler about who had been responsible for letting the lawman escape. He nudged the horse ahead, breathing a bit more easily after he'd passed the cave entrance. A few more yards brought him to the bodies. He reined in beside Haven's lifeless form.

A glance was enough to tell him that his Colt was not in the outlaw's dead hand or stuck into his belt. He had not thought that Dorsey would pass the gun on to anyone else.

116

Toeing his horse ahead, he reined in beside Dorsey's recumbent body. Aside from the Smith & Wesson .41 that lay close to the dead man's outstretched right hand, there was no sign of another weapon.

It looks like he wasn't figuring to use a strange gun, either, Longarm told himself silently. *So there ain't but one other place to look, and that's in Dorsey's saddlebags.*

Touching his horse's side with his toe, Longarm rode on past the corpses to the horses Dorsey and Haven had been riding. Dorsey's mount stood quietly, twenty or thirty feet beyond the bodies.

Longarm did not dismount when he reached the animal, but leaned out to lift the saddlebags off its rump. When he thrust his hand into the side of the bags nearest to him, Longarm felt only yielding cloth and a packet of some kind. He turned the bag around and the first object his fingers encountered was the familiar butt of his own Colt. He lifted it out, glanced at the base of the cylinder, and saw that it was still fully loaded.

Old son, Longarm told himself, *this is just the medicine you need to go back and take charge of them scoundrels in the cave. There ain't likely to be no better time, seeing as they're likely still upset and fussing at each other.*

Reining his horse around, Longarm started back along the canyon toward the mouth of the gypsum cave. As he slid the familiar Colt back into its holster, Longarm felt as though he'd just been reunited with a long-lost friend. He threw the saddlebags over his shoulder and turned the horse back in the direction of the cave.

He was in no special hurry. He let the animal walk while he returned his attention to the contents of the saddlebag. The oblong packet had aroused his curiosity, and he took it out first. It was a sturdy manila envelope, the flap unsealed. A glance inside showed him the envelope was crammed with currency wrapped in half a dozen sheets of folded papers. Longarm whistled as he looked at the thickness of the bundle. He was holding fifty or sixty thousand dollars.

He dropped the bulky sheaf of currency in his own saddle-bag and was lifting the other papers out to examine them when

117

the thudding of hoofbeats and the creaking of wagon wheels reached his ears. Glancing ahead and then turning to look behind, he saw nothing moving along the canyon floor in either direction. He realized then that the wagon he heard must be traveling along its rim. Tilting his head, he saw the curve of its canvas top looming against the now-bright sky. The edge of the canyon wall hid the driver from him.

Suddenly Longarm remembered that he was in strange country, and in an area that drew only the few travelers who were forced to cross the virtually waterless expanse of Frenchman Flat. He reined his horse over until it huddled against the sheer canyon wall, where he could not be seen at a casual glance. After he had pulled up the horse, crowding the animal as close as possible to the sheer wall, he heard the creaking of the wagon's axles and the grinding of its wheels. Then the vehicle came to a halt directly above his head.

Certain that he had been discovered, Longarm quickly draped the outlaw's saddle bags over his horse's rump and drew his rifle. He held the gun ready to level it, knowing that he'd pumped a shell into the chamber when he reloaded after the fracas by the cave. Then a man's voice from the wagon above him broke the silence.

"Damn it, by now we ought've already hit that cut that'll take us down into the bottom of the wash," he said.

Since the man had raised his voice almost to a shout, Longarm judged that he must have directed his remark to somebody who was quite a distance from him.

"You wanta set here and rest the hosses while I send a man to ride ahead and see how much farther we got to go?" a second man's voice called. This speaker's voice was raised, too.

"Hell, maybe we better send a rider both ways," the first man replied. "For all I know, that place might be in the other direction from the one we turned in. Maybe we been going the wrong way, and it's in back of us."

"Not likely," a third voice chimed in. "I'd bet dollars to doughnuts the cave we're looking for has gotta be up ahead of us. Remember, Jimson said the place where we can get the wagon down into the canyon lays just beyond the cave."

"He did, at that," the first speaker agreed. "He told us the—" The racuous braying of a mule drowned the man's voice. After the mule's harsh vocalizing ended, the speaker was saying "He said that when we get to the bottom all we've got to do is go straight on in the direction we'll be heading until we spot the cave. Said we can't miss it."

"Well, damn it all!" the second man broke in. "We been going alongside this gulch since daybreak, but we still ain't seen no place like Jimson told us about."

"You're right about that," one of the others agreed. "I tell you the truth, all I'm sure about right now is that this gully we're following is the one they call the Vegas Wash."

"You fellows know the country around here better'n I do," the wagon driver said. "Let's go on a ways farther, mebbe another half-mile or so. If we don't run into that place we're looking for before then, we better send some scouts out in both directions."

When Longarm had heard the first part of the conversation between the men on the rim, he'd been tempted for a moment to call to them and tell them that the trail down into the wash still lay ahead of them. Upon hearing the cavern mentioned, he cursed himself mentally for having failed to realize at once that the wagon with its outriders had been dispatched by the same individuals who had sent Dorsey, Haven, and Sadler to join the Apache Kid and Annie.

As a precaution, he drew his Winchester from its scabbard and cradled it in the crook of one arm when he heard the hooves of the draft mules that pulled the wagon thudding on the ground as the driver started them moving again. The sounds made by the wagon did not drown the soft thuds of the hooves of several horses that were accompanying it.

Staying motionless, Longarm listened to the shrill creaking noises of the wagon and the thuds of hoofbeats that drifted down through the quiet air into the wash. He tried to determine how many riders were in the group on the rim. The noises made by the horses were confused and intermingled with those of the mules pulling the wagon. On the rim of the wash as on its floor the ground was so soft and sandy and so muffling in its effect that his usually keen ear could tell only that there was more than two horsemen and fewer than half a dozen riding with the wagon.

Keeping his ears attuned to the noises made by the wagon and its outriders until the sounds were swallowed by distance into the silence of the desert, Longarm took stock of the situation into which his chase had led him.

Now, them fellows was sent here to help Dorsey and the other, Longarm told himself silently as he waited for the noise of the wagon and its outriders to fade. *That's why all that money's in these saddlebags, to pay 'em off with, and maybe to buy some of Apache Annie's Indian friends to help 'em. But there's just too damn many of 'em for you to handle by yourself, old son. They ain't going to pay no attention to your badge.*

Them fellows Annie told you about really means business or they wouldn't've sent these men here. They aim to chase Bart Calder's survey crew off the job or wipe 'em out once and for all, and from what I know about Calder, he ain't a man that's gonna lay down and play dead and let somebody shovel dirt over him. No, sir. Calder's the kind that fights back.

It sorta looks like you got yourself pushed right into the middle of a war, and that's one hell of a uncomfortable place for a man to get shoved into. There ain't much use fighting a war when you ain't got enough cartridges to put the other side outa action. And even if you had enough bullets, it's a lot more important to get word to Bart Calder what's happening around here right now. There ain't no use in fighting if you ain't got the shells you need to win.

Replacing the rifle in its scabbard, Longarm turned his horse and started in the opposite direction to that taken by the wagon. The sun had risen high enough by now to flood one side wall of the wash with its rays. For the first half-hour or so the slow rise in temperature did not bother Longarm. Then, as the blazing sun climbed higher and its heat was reflected from the deep coating of almost sheer white sand that covered the canyon floor, the air started shimmering and grew hotter and hotter.

Soon Longarm began sweating, and the livery horse

slowed its pace. It started heaving now and then and sweat began pouring through its coat. Longarm looked for a spot of shade, but there was none. He kept the reins taut, pulling back on them to keep the horse at the slowest walk possible. The animal's breathing eased for a short while and its rib-barrel stopped pulsing each time it breathed, but the relief was only temporary and soon its sides began heaving again.

Because the deep layer of soft white sand that lay over the long-dry riverbed swallowed hoofbeats the way the toad's mouth swallows an insect, Longarm did not hear the two riders coming up behind him. His first knowledge that he was being followed came from his horse. He had reined in to let it rest when it suddenly twitched its ears nervously, stamped on the baking hot sand, and twisted its neck, trying to look behind it.

Longarm frowned. The horse's actions meant that there was another horse in the vicinity, and his mount had responded in a reflex to the herd instinct so deeply inbred in all horses that no amount of training could banish it completely.

Twisting in the saddle, Longarm looked back, but he had reached the point at which the wash began to narrow and describe a wide curve. Both ahead of him and behind him his vision was very sharply limited. He sat quietly, attuning his ears to the almost total silence of the flats on either side of the wash, but he heard nothing. The air was absolutely still. Not even a rustle came from the sagebrush that stretched back from the rim of the gully and covered Frenchman Flat.

All the same, there's got to be somebody dogging along on your tracks, old son, Longarm told himself silently. *And you don't need to do a lot of figuring to narrow it down real quick. Them fellows in the wagon finally got connected up with Apache Annie and the Kid and that hired gunman that was sent up here with them other two.*

After a while they must've got things sorted out and missed Dorsey's saddlebags, which ain't a bit strange, because you toted 'em away absent-minded like after you went through 'em. If they'd found out the money is gone, they'd've been after you before now. But by now they've likely figured out what must've happened, and sent somebody after you.

121

It'd be Sadler and the Apache Kid, most likely. Whoever it is, they're getting too close for comfort. You better cut a shuck outa here, old son. Chances are you could outshoot whoever's after you, but the main job you got is to get back to Bart Calder's survey outfit and let 'em know there's trouble coming. They're bound to have some way of getting word to Calder that they need help.

First job you got, though, is to slow down whoever's coming after you. Looks like the best way's to give 'em a little bit of bait to chew on.

Shifting in the saddle, Longarm picked up the outlaw's saddlebags and took a last quick look at their contents. As nearly as he could tell, his Colt and the fat envelope full of money had been the only things they'd ever held except Dover's personal stuff. He buckled the flap straps and tossed the bags out into the center of the wash's sandy floor, where the men who were chasing him could not miss spotting them. Then he nudged his horse again to urge the tiring animal ahead and continued toward the mouth of the dry wash.

Once again Longarm twisted in the saddle and looked behind him. The sheer high curving walls of the wash still hid him from whoever was chasing him. He realized that the wait he'd had to make in order to avoid being discovered by the wagon train could very well be a costly one. He was surprised at how little distance he'd covered since passing the cavern door. He could still see the saddlebags, a dark brown blob against the white expanse of sand that covered the floor of the wash.

Them saddlebags of Dorsey's oughta buy you a little bit of time, old son, he thought. *Them fellows coming up the wash is sure to be looking for 'em, because they knew he was carrying all that money. They'll likely stop and look to see if it's still inside 'em. That'll give you time to get a start on 'em, because once they find the money ain't there they'll figure out who's taken it, and start chasing after you.*

Though the distance still ahead of him seemed interminable, only a quarter of an hour passed before Longarm rode out of the steep confining walls of the big curving gully. He'd kept his ears pitched for noises from behind him, but so far had heard nothing. He was sure the riders behind him had stopped to examine the saddlebags, giving him a chance to increase his lead.

Emerging from the wash, he welcomed even the scanty cover provided by the low-growing sagebrush that covered the featureless, level expanse of Frenchman Flat. Less than a quarter of a mile away, Longarm saw a small herd of wild horses grazing lazily. Even at such a short distance their individual forms were indistinct, distorted by the shimmering heat haze.

By now the sun was high in the sky and moving steadily toward its zenith. Its rays still poured down their blistering heat, but the low-growing sage bushes shielded the ground and kept it from reflecting the sunshine as had the white sand on the bed of the wash. A light breeze rustled through the tops of the sagebrush now and then and brought occasional relief from the heat.

There ain't but one thing wrong with this damn country that a few trees wouldn't cure, old son, Longarm mused silently as he squinted up at the sun to get a bearing on the direction he needed to take to get back to the survey camp. *They'd give a man a place to take cover when he's got a couple of outlaws hot on his trail. Why, the tops of them brushes is so low that a man'd have to be laying flat on his back before they hid him.*

He'd covered only a few dozen yards when the significance of what he'd just been thinking gave him the idea.

"Flat on his back," he repeated aloud. "Laying down flat, that sagebrush oughta make real good cover, thick as it grows here. Except there ain't no way to wrassle the horse down, and it'd be a dead giveaway."

He rode on a bit farther before the second idea struck him and he reined in.

"When you can't hide something, all you can do is make it look like what it ain't, old son," Longarm said into the empty air. "There's enough wild horses roaming around here so that nobody'd pay much attention to a stray. And that's about the only chance you got, so there ain't a damned thing to lose by giving it a try."

Longarm wasted no time in putting his hastily improvised scheme into action. He dropped from the saddle and took his Winchester from its sheath. He pulled free the ties holding his saddlebags and placed them on the ground beside the rifle. The girth strap was his next job. He freed it quickly by yanking free the knot which held it in the iron ring that connected it to the saddle leathers. The heavy braids of the *cincha* dropped to the ground, and he lifted the McClellan saddle together with its harness straps and his rifle scabbard from the horse's back. It was the work of only a moment to unbuckle the headstall and drop it to the ground beside the saddle along with the bridle and bit.

As he worked, the noise of hoofbeats coming from the direction of the wash had grown steadily louder.

"Them fellows is going to be here in just about two more minutes, old son," Longarm muttered under his breath. "Damned if this ain't the craziest scheme you ever tried. If it don't work, and whoever that is chasing after you spooks this nag, you're sure gonna be up shit creek without no paddle. But it's the only game going, and you got to play whatever cards you got, even if they don't make up such a much of a hand."

Chapter 13

Longarm dropped flat into the concealment of the low-growing sage and reached for his rifle. Then he cocked his ears toward the sounds of hoofbeats from the big gully, which grew louder minute by minute. Though he was unable to see the riders, his ears told him there were two sets of hoofbeats. Within a few more minutes the sound of the approaching horses changed. The thudding of their hooves was no longer muffled and soft, but resonated with solid thunks as the animals carried their riders off the soft yielding sand that covered the bottom of Vegas Wash and stepped onto the hard-baked soil of Frenchman Flat.

For a few moments the drumming of the hoofbeats grew louder as the horsemen neared Longarm. For a moment he thought they were going to pass him and ride on, but before they reached the spot where he was hiding they stopped abruptly. Longarm judged the men were within eighty or ninety yards of him when they reined in.

Accustomed to thinking of distance in such circumstances

in terms of bullets, Longarm decided they were a bit too far to assure him of accurate shooting with his Colt, and decided the circumstances called for him to use his rifle if a showdown developed.

"Damn it!" one of the riders grated, his voice gravelly-rough. "Unless Apache Annie and that boy of hers and Sadler all three lied to us about when they seen the Longarm son of a bitch last, he can't've traveled far enough to be outa sight yet!"

"You sure don't see no signs of him, do you?" the other man asked. "Level as this country is, we'd spot him sure if he was anyplace close by."

Both voices were strange to Longarm.

"Hell, Karnes, you don't have to tell me that," the rough-voiced man snapped. "I got my own eyes, they're as good as yours."

"I guess you see that nag standing over there, then," the man called Karnes went on. "Don't it strike you strange that there'd be a lone horse out here?"

"Not a bit," the nameless rider replied. "There's wild horses all over Frenchman Flat. This is where the redskins comes to catch 'em. If you'll look over to the north yonder a little ways you'll see the herd that one come from."

"Just the same, maybe we oughta ride over and take a look at it," Karnes suggested. "That critter looks too big to me to be a wild horse. They're mostly kinda runty."

"You go if you want to," his companion said. "But you'd just be wasting your time. Chances are that Long's back-tracked on hisself and went the other way outa the wash. I'm betting that's just what he done."

"Not likely," Karnes replied. "That's the way we come in, remember. All the time we was riding along the rim of that gulch with the wagon, we could see down into the bottom of it. If Long had of been in the wash, we'd've spotted him for sure."

"There ain't no such thing as sure in this damn country, and especially when you're looking for somebody as cagey as they say this Longarm fellow is."

"Bullshit, Jernigan!" Karnes snorted. "Long might be

cagey, all right, but he puts on his pants one leg at a time, just the same as you and me!"

"That's as may be," Jernigan answered. His voice showed his impatience.

Longarm now had learned the names of both the men. He had never heard of either one before, but it had been quite a while since his last case out in Nevada. He tucked their names away in his mind for future reference and resisted the temptation to lift his head above the tops of the sagebrush to get a clear look at them.

Jernigan went on, "I was half way sure we'd catch up with him before we got this far. I been hearing about this Longarm for such a long time that I'd sorta like to run into him. He's put two or three damn good men I've rode with under six feet of dirt, and I got a hunch I just might be the one that can out-shoot him."

Karnes said, "Well, it don't look like you'll get to find out this time around. But if Long did go the other way outa the wash, the Major and Fat Jaw'll run him down. That big-bellied Apache renegade's the best tracker I ever seen."

"Sure," Jernigan replied, "but it's bound to be like I said. If Long had've come this way, we'd've seen him. There sure ain't no place where he could be hiding."

At that moment the livery horse decided it was ready to move again. It whuffled and started to turn. Longarm grabbed for a hind hoof as the animal lifted it to move. That was the only way he could think of to stop the animal from going too far without standing up where the gunslingers could see him. His clutching fingers brushed against the hard shell of the hoof, but he was short by an inch of being able to close his hand and grasp it. The horse completed its turn. Then, as suddenly as it had started moving, the animal stopped and stood motionless again.

Although the horse's shift in position had covered less than a yard of actual distance, its unexpected movement had spoiled Longarm's improvised ruse in hiding, as he learned quickly when one of the outlaws spoke.

"Hold on!" Karnes said. "That ain't no wild horse! It's got a brand on it!"

"Damned if you ain't right!" Jernigan agreed. "I can't make out what it is from here, but I can sure see the mark."

"I never heard of a horse going wild again once it's been broke and rode," Karnes said. "Now, I ain't as anxious as you been to catch up with Long, but now that we've run across that horse, I got me a hunch that's just what we've done. That's bound to be his horse, which means he's in spitting distance of us right now!"

"Then he's got to be holed up in that sagebrush someplace close to the horse!" Jernigan snapped. "I'll dust the bastard out so we can get him in our sights!"

Almost before the outlaw had finished speaking, his rifle barked and a bullet thunked into the hard dirt a foot away from Longarm. Too combat-wise to fire or even to raise his head and shoulders above the low-growing sage to aim, Longarm did not move or stir. He knew his enemies would be watching closely and that any rustling of the sagebrush would draw their fire.

"Damn it, you're wasting bullets!" Karnes snapped as the echo of his companion's shot died away. "You got about as much chance as a snowball in hell of hitting anybody or anything that's hiding in the sage with wild shots like that! All you're doing is telling Longarm where to aim!"

"I don't need to tell him!" Jernigan replied. "Wherever he's scooted down, chances are pretty good he can see us a lot better'n we can see him! Anyways, if that's his horse, he's gotta be someplace close to it."

"Close covers a lot of territory," Karnes pointed out. "But talking about close, if we're bunched up together this way, he can cut both of us down with a couple of quick shots. We better split up, Jernigan."

"That suits me. The smart thing for us to do is get him between us. Then we can catch him in a crossfire."

"You angle off down below the horse, then," Karnes told his companion. "I'll give you a start. Then I'll head across between that lone nag and the mustang herd. That way we'll have Longarm between us."

In his place of scanty concealment, Longarm could hear his enemies quite clearly as they made their plans. He did not like what he'd just heard. He risked raising his head, sure that the gunmen would be so busy picking their way to new positions that they would fail to notice him.

When his eyes were above the tops of the low-growing sage, he saw that he'd been right. Jernigan was reining his mount around, and Longarm saw that the gunman's plan was to ride parallel to the rim of the wash, where he could then circle back to cover the area Longarm would have to traverse when he started across the flat.

Karnes had not yet put his horse into motion. He was watching Jernigan, his eyes turned away from Longarm's position. The wild mustang herd had been moving slowly toward the mouth of the wash as the animals grazed. They were closer now than they had been when Longarm's pursuers caught up with him.

If the positions of the three men and the horse herd had been plotted on paper with connecting lines, the lines would have formed a long slim triangle, like that of a tall church steeple, with the wild horse herd at its tip. A slanting line from Longarm to the herd would have marked one side and another long slanting line from the herd to the moving Jernigan would have been the second.

Karnes would have been outside the second line, which was growing steadily longer as Jernigan drew closer to Longarm. The third line that would form the triangle's base also grew longer as Jernigan got farther from Karnes and continued to ride parallel to the bank of the wash. This third line formed the base of the triangle.

Quickly, Longarm calculated his chances. The distances between his two targets was the complicating problem. He did not make the mistake of underestimating his enemies. He knew that both of them were professional gunfighters, skilled in the use of their weapons. He had no chance of getting off two telling shots before the surviving gunman cut him down.

If he shot Jernigan, Longarm knew that Karnes could trigger off at least one shot before he could swing his Winchester to bring him down. The result would be the same if he chose Karnes as his first target. While the muzzle of his Winchester was traversing the long arc that would bring Jernigan into his sights, Jernigan would have plenty of time to aim and fire.

Then, in a split second, Longarm saw his opportunity. He needed to kill or at least disable both Karnes and Jernigan in order to have the time he needed to saddle his horse if he was to escape being caught in a crossfire between the two outlaws. He saw that there was only an outside chance of his instantly conceived scheme working, but he had no other choice.

It's a long shot in more ways than one, old son, he thought. But it's the only one you got.

Longarm lifted his head above the tops of the sage bushes while he was bringing up his rifle. He saw that Jernigan was almost opposite him now. The gunman was still riding steadily along the rim of the wash. Karnes was watching Jernigan, waiting for his companion to get into position. The wild mustang herd had not moved.

Springing to his feet and spreading them to steady himself as he moved, Longarm let off two quick shots. He did not aim at either of the gunmen. Actually, he had no single target, but placed his slugs to crease either of the three wild horses that stood at its fringes on the side farthest from the wash.

Longarm did not wait to see the result of his shots, but dropped flat on the ground again. As the throaty, air-shattering scream of the mustang he'd hit burst out to fill the air, he was cramming two fresh shells into the rifle's magazine to replace the ones he'd used.

It took Longarm only a few seconds to insert the fresh cartridges. The scream of the wounded horse still hung in the air. The last notes of the mustang's cry were drowned by the pounding of hoofbeats on the stone-hard earth. The hoofbeats told him that his slug had done its work, and the wild horses were stampeding.

Longarm heard Karnes shout Jernigan's name before the noise of the hoofbeats shut out all other sounds. What Jernigan said, and what Karnes replied—if indeed he replied at all—was lost in the noise of the wild herd's pounding hoofbeats. Certain that the mustangs' unexpected movements would be holding the outlaws' attention for a few more seconds, Longarm raised his head above the tops of the sagebrush for a look.

Karnes was still sitting his horse, staring at the lead horses of the stampeding herd as the panicked animals drew near him. Longarm looked for Jernigan, and saw him turning his horse away from the rim of the wash to get out of the way before the crazed horses got close. Neither was looking at Longarm.

Jernigan was the nearest target. Longarm brought up his rifle and got the outlaw in his sights. He triggered off the shot, and as the slug hit Jernigan he lurched sideways on his horse. The outlaw almost fell, but managed to pull himself erect in the saddle again. His left hand was dangling by his side, but it still grasped his rifle.

When Longarm saw that Jernigan would be unable to respond to his shot, he felt a momentary temptation to trigger off the slug that would put the outlaw out of the fight permanently, but his combat sense warned him that with one of the killers out of the action it was more urgent to turn his attention to the second gunman and to his own horse.

As he twisted around to look for Karnes, Longarm glimpsed the stampeding horse herd. The herd was now strung out and streaming across the flat. Even in the short time that had elapsed, the half-dozen wild horses in the lead were within a dozen yards of passing Karnes and hiding Longarm from him.

You better not lallygag around no more with them gunmen, old son, Longarm told himself. *Jernigan's hurt bad and Karnes ain't going to get a bead on you before them horses gets between us. What you'd best do quick as you can is get that nag of yours saddled and ready to ride again.*

As Longarm turned away, Karnes's rifle barked. The slug whistled over Longarm's head to kick up a small shower of clods from the baked soil beyond the livery house. The instinct for survival that had kept him alive through so many such showdowns warned Longarm to shoot back. He swivelled quickly, shouldering his Winchester as he turned, and snapshotted.

His shot was almost unaimed. The slug from the rifle flew too low to put Karnes out of the action. Instead, it thunked into the shoulder of the outlaw's horse and met the hard bone

131

of the beast's shoulder. Deflected by the bone, the slug's energy took it into the horse's neck and severed the animal's jugular vein.

Spurting great gouts of blood, the horse swayed for only a few seconds before its legs folded. It fell heavily, catapulting Karnes to the ground. The outlaw's rifle spun out of his hands and cartwheeled through the air. The weapon dropped to earth far out of Karnes's reach. The outlaw hit the ground heavily, lay stunned for a moment, then began crawling toward the rifle.

By this time the leaders of the stampeding horse herd had come abreast of Karnes. Longarm was shifting his aim to get the downed outlaw in his sights when the first of the horses came between him and his target, blotting out his sight of the man on the ground. Realizing that he now had several minutes before Karnes would be back into action, Longarm glanced quickly at Jernigan. The wounded man was still struggling to raise his rifle and succeeding no better than before.

Accustomed as he was to making instant judgments, Longarm started for the livery horse on a run. The animal had not strayed after its first movement away from him. Longarm grabbed up his saddle trappings as he came to them and took full advantage of the protective cover provided by the wild horses to fling the saddle on his mount's back and draw the *cincha* tight around its belly.

Taking another quick glance toward the outlaws, he saw that the stampeding wild horse herd had raised so much dust from the baked desert soil that he could see neither of his antagonists. The dust hung heavy, roiling into clouds in the dry hot air, forming a shielding screen between Longarm and the outlaws.

Longarm tossed his saddlebags on the horse's rump, freeing his hands of everything except his rifle and the horse's reins. As he reached the animal's head, carrying the rifle in one hand and the beast's headstall and reins in the other, he looked again toward the two gunmen. Though the last of the spooked horses were straggling by between him and his antagonists, the dust cloud raised by their stampede still hung thickly enough to screen his moves.

132

With a few quick motions of his experienced fingers, Longarm slid the bit into the horse's mouth and tightened the straps of the headstall. He took still another look around after he had swung into his saddle. The dust cloud had begun to thin out as it settled. Through its dancing motes he could see that Karnes had apparently given up the idea of carrying on with the attack, for he was running toward Jernigan.

There was still a good distance between the two, but Jernigan had managed to turn his horse now. He was starting toward his fellow outlaw. Jernigan's wounded arm was still dangling loosely at his side, but he had managed to slide his rifle into its saddle scabbard.

They ain't going to bother you much, old son, the shape they're in now, Longarm told himself silently.

He found the stirrup with his boot toe and was swinging into the saddle when the sharp bark of a rifle and the muted thunk of a bullet into the hard soil at one side of him proved that his optimistic thought had been wrong. As he settled into the saddle, Longarm turned to look at the outlaws again.

Karnes had stopped running. He'd dropped to one knee and was leveling his rifle again.

"Damned if he ain't got a lot of stick-to-it," Longarm muttered.

Leaning forward in the saddle, Longarm flattened himself along the horse's shoulder. Karnes's rifle spoke as he moved, and the slug the outlaw had intended for the lawman whistled angrily through empty air.

Jernigan was within a few feet of Karnes now. Longarm was in no position to get off a quick shot. His horse was facing away from the two outlaws. During the few moments required for Longarm to wheel his mount and raised his Winchester, Jernigan reached his dismounted companion. Karnes was leaping to the rump of Jernigan's mount when Longarm's horse completed its turn and he could once more get the outlaws in the Winchester's sights.

He fired, but the rump of a retreating horse carrying two men who were both bending forward along the animal's back presented a target that was too small even for Longarm's expert shooting. His slug was off the mark. It kicked up a spurt of dust from the ground beyond the fleeing gunmen.

By the time Longarm had levered a fresh round into the chamber, the horse carrying the fleeing outlaws was in full gallop. Its rump was bobbing up and down, the two riders still crouching forward, stretching along its back.

Longarm tried to hold his sights on target, swinging the Winchester's muzzle from side to side. Each time that he had the retreating men in the vee of his sights the horse veered before he could trigger off the shot. By the time he had corrected his aim, the animal was on another course, veering away again.

"Them fellows has been shot at too many times before," Longarm muttered as he watched the outlaws disappearing into the Vegas Wash. "They was smart enough to run when they seen they didn't have a chance. But there'll be another day, and it won't turn out as good for 'em. It ain't smart to chase 'em now. The thing you got to do is cut a shuck back to that survey camp and get Jared's crew ready for the bunch that's down in the wash."

Longarm turned his mount and toed it ahead. Trailed by the thin line of smoke from his cheroot, he set off across Frenchman Flat.

Chapter 14

Longarm was surprised at first by the short ride that was necessary before he crossed the trail of the survey party. Sunset was still more than an hour away when he sighted the first of the stakes that Foster's crews were setting. Then he realized that he had been able to return in a straight line, where as he had done a lot of zigging and zagging over the prairie when searching for the Apache Kid. Later, he'd taken an even more circuitous course when he tracked the Kid to the cave in the Vegas Wash.

Though he hadn't known exactly where the survey party was located, all that he'd needed to do was to ride southwest from the wash until he came in sight of one of the tall stakes with its fluttering ribbons, then follow the line of stakes until he came to the spot where the party was camped.

There was still daylight left when he saw the canvas top of a wagon ahead. As he drew closer he could see one of the men on the survey crew loading his transit in the wagon, but he could not identify him at once. A few paces from the wagon, a bright red streamer fluttered from the top of a tall stake. The stake glowed with the bright yellow of fresh wood. The man at the wagon saw Longarm, stared a moment, then waved. Longarm was close enough now to recognize him as Jared Foster.

"We were wondering at breakfast this morning where you'd got off to," Foster said as Longarm reined in. "None of us figured you'd be gone more than overnight. I hope you didn't run into a lot of trouble."

"Oh, there was a couple of dustups, but they wasn't too big for me to handle," Longarm replied.

"By dustups you mean shooting?"

"I used up a few shells," Longarm admitted. He swung out of the saddle and kicked his feet into the sandy soil beside the wagon to get the stiffness out of his knees.

"Did you settle anything, or will we still have more trouble up ahead?"

"Well, I ain't fool enough to say there won't be no more trouble before you get the last stakes set."

"That doesn't sound so good," Foster commented. "We've still got a lot of ground to cover. It's pretty easy to see that you haven't been lallygagging around since you left the crew. You look like you could use a square meal."

Longarm nodded. "I been too busy to do more'n snatch a bite on the run since I left."

"You're thirsty, too, I expect," Foster suggested. "Help yourself from my barrel, if you are."

Longarm shook his head. "I never did hurt for drinking water, but a square meal and a bath and a shave would do me a lot of good, if you got enough water in the barrels."

"I'm sure there's plenty for a sponge-off and a shave," Foster said. "We filled up good before we left Mormon Wells, and there ought to be enough water in the big barrel to hold us until we get to the next place we can fill up."

"Then, if you ain't in too big of a rush, I'll just strip down and sponge off right here and now," Longarm suggested.

"I'm afraid you'll have to wait until we catch up with Hobbs and Brown. The big barrel's in their wagon. I just carry enough in mine to drink and give the horse what it needs when there's no water holes handy. But they can't be too far ahead

136

of us. And the others will be coming in pretty soon. I whipped up to get a lead on them, but they aren't too far behind. We'll be having supper when they pull in."

"I'll just ride alongside of you while we're catching up, then," Longarm suggested. "You can spot them stakes a lot easier than me, and I might even shut my eyes a time or two and let 'em rest from all the glare they been in."

"I've been keeping track, and I don't think there'll be more than one stake, maybe two, before we catch up with Hobbs and Brown," Foster said. He slapped the reins over his horse's back and the wagon rolled ahead.

Longarm nudged his mount with a toe and the horse stepped along. They rode in silence for a short distance. Then Longarm said, "Since I been seeing all them stakes your outfit's setting, I got a question to put to you."

"Ask away."

"If somebody was to go along and pull up all them stakes you been setting, how long would it take for you to get new ones down?"

For a moment the survey foreman stared at Longarm, his mouth open and his brows knitted. "Are you telling me somebody has been messing with our line stakes?" he asked.

"Not yet, they ain't. But it just come to me while I was following 'em on my way back here that it wouldn't be much of a job for a couple of men to ride along a day or so behind you and pull them stakes outa the ground."

"That'd sure raise hell, all right," Foster said slowly. "I never had it happen on any job I was on. Oh, a time or two some redskin riding past our lines will pull the cloth off of a few of 'em. I guess the Indians use them for headbands and belly-ties. You know how much they like red. Taking the cloth streamer away doesn't hurt us, but if they pull the stake up we have to go back and shoot the grade again to fill in the gap."

Longarm shook his head. "I ain't talking about one or two stakes, Foster. I'm asking what'd happen if somebody rode down your line from one end to the other and pulled up every one of the stakes you'd set since you started."

"That'd run to a real job," Foster said slowly. "We'd just have to start from scratch and survey the whole line again."

137

"I sorta figured that's what you'd say," Longarm nodded. "And how long would it take?"

"Just about as long as it did to set the line the first time. Oh, sure, we keep notes as we go along, but they don't take the place of the stakes. Those stakes are what a railroad construction boss goes by when he lays out the line for the tracks."

"You mean he'd need the stakes even if he had them notes?"

"Sure," the surveyor replied. "I don't suppose you've ever taken a close look at one of our stakes. Before we drive in a stake we mark it with longitude, latitude, elevation, and grade. Our notes wouldn't help a construction boss much unless he could also read the notes on the stakes."

"And how long did you say you been on this job?"

"Going on eight months. A survey team can only move so fast, even over ground that's good and level. Which I don't have to tell you isn't exactly the way it's been in most of the ground we've covered before we hit Frenchman Flat."

"Well, don't look so worried, Foster," Longarm told the foreman. "I just followed your stakes till I caught up with you, and on the way I got to thinking about what would happen if somebody was to come along and yank all of 'em out and toss 'em on a fire."

"If all you were doing was wondering what would happen, I feel better already," Foster said. "Losing almost a year of work would really set this job way back."

"Nobody's been pulling up your survey stakes yet," Longarm assured him. "Leastways, not that I noticed while I was guiding myself by 'em."

"That's good news," Foster said with a smile. Then his face grew sober as he looked more closely at Longarm. "But from the kind of questions you've been asking me, I've got a hunch there's some bad news coming."

"Things can't always look good," Longarm said slowly. "I still got one or two more questions I need answered before we go any further."

"I'll do the best I can. Go ahead."

138

Longarm wasted no time. "You ever hear of a fellow called the Major?"

"If you're talking about Major Pawley, I sure as hell have!" Foster replied. "And I guess it's him you mean, because he's the only one I know that folks call that."

"I figured you might've heard about him," Longarm nodded.

"So has just about everybody else in the state of Nevada, and I guess in some parts of Arizona and California, too."

"From the way you said that, I figure he's got quite a reputation," Longarm said dryly. "Gunfighter, is he?"

"He hired his gun when he first showed up out here, or so I've heard," Foster nodded. "He's supposed to've been with Quantrill's old gang when he wasn't anything but a kid. I understand he just . . . Well, as far as I know, he just turned up out here in Nevada right after the War."

"That sounds to me like it ain't much but saloon talk." Longarm frowned. "Did you ever get anything direct from this Major himself?"

"I've met him, but that's all. I just happened to be standing next to him at the Oasis Bar in Carson City and the barkeep introduced us," Foster replied. "I said hello and goodbye to him and that's as far as we got."

"Looks like I'll have to settle for hearing about his reputation, then." Longarm frowned thoughtfully. "Tell me what else you've heard."

It was Foster's turn to frown. "Folks say he got here by way of Tombstone and Bodie and a few other places," the surveyor said slowly. "But I don't believe anybody knows for sure. I've heard he was a sheriff or a city marshal or something like that back in Texas, but I'd have a hard time recalling who told me that. He's supposed to've started out as a saloon gambler who killed a few men when they called him for cheating. Then I guess he figured he could make more hiring his gun than he could dealing cards."

"All that sounds pretty much like saloon chatter," Longarm said thoughtfully. "But I guess the only man in Nevada that could tell me the real story is this Major Pawley himself."

"And from what I've heard, you might or might not get any answer," Foster told him. "But you can ask some of the other fellows when we're all together. And that ought not to be too long, because unless I'm mistaken, that's the big wagon right up ahead of us."

"We're getting here just about at the right time, too," Longarm said. He looked at the sky. The fading sunshine of the dying desert day was gone and the eastern sky was shading into the deep blue of night. "I don't mind saying that bath we was talking about and a hot supper won't make me a bit mad."

"You go on and bathe as soon as we stop, then," Foster suggested. "I've got to go over the day's work with Hobbs and Brown, and as soon as the other wagons pull in we'll be starting to cook."

Sitting on the tailgate of the big lead wagon, which he had dropped level with the wagonbed, Longarm levered out of his boots. Turning them sole-up, he shook and tapped them to get rid of the irritating grains of sand they had accumulated during his stay in the cave and in the Vegas Wash.

Old son, he told himself as he worked, *there might be grittier places in this world than you been during the last few days, but if there is, you ain't come across 'em yet. And what's more, you don't ever want to.*

Stripping, he shook his clothes to dislodge the grit that had accumulated around the garments' seams and creases. Then, with the clothing placed out of his way, Longarm splashed water from his cupped hands over his muscular frame and rubbed away the gritty remnants that adhered to his body.

This here's a long ways from stretching out in hot water all the way up to your neck, but there likely ain't no bathtubs in this whole stretch of land south of the Comstock, he mused as he washed. *Anyhow, you ain't got the time to waste soaking yourself. That crowd of plug-uglies sure as hell won't be wasting their time taking baths, even if there was a tub up there for every man jack of 'em.*

His quick washing completed, Longarm dug a fresh cheroot from his vest pocket and lighted it while he propped his heels up on the wagon-gate and sat in the warm pre-sunset

140

breeze that was just springing up, waiting for it to dry him. The long slim cigar was still only half-smoked, and he had put on his clothing except for his vest when the rumble of wheels reached his ears.

He slid his arms into the vest, jogged his gunbelt to get it set just right, and started toward Foster's wagon just in time to see the other wagons pulling up. Sarah Roundtree was handling the reins, with Cross sitting beside her.

Sarah saw Longarm at the same time he saw her. She handed the reins to Cross and before the wagon had stopped moving she'd jumped to the ground and was running to greet him.

"Longarm!" she said as she threw her arms around him. "You've been gone so long that I was getting real worried about you! Where on earth have you been?"

"Not awful far, Sarah," he replied. "But you'll hear all about it later, when I tell Jared Foster and the others about what we're likely to run into."

"I guess I'm just about as glad as Sarah is to see you, Marshal Long," Cross put in as he came up to them. "Seems like since you rode off, Sarah hasn't let more'n five minutes go by without asking me if I think you're all right."

"You and her can both see for yourselves that I'm healthy as I'll ever be," Longarm said. "Except I'm getting a mite hungry, and I guess you are, too."

"We certainly are!" Sarah agreed. "It hasn't taken me long to find out that working on a survey crew gives me a lot bigger appetite than I ever had doing housework. But the others can't be far behind us, so we'll be fixing supper pretty soon."

"Then let's walk on over to the campfire," Longarm suggested. "While we're fixing supper, I'll save us all time by telling everybody what I've found out,"

"It's too bad you didn't have a chance to count those men you ran into at the Vegas Wash," Jared Foster frowned as he spoke for the first time after Longarm finished filling in the group on his encounter.

Longarm had told his companions of his experiences while

141

they ate supper. Now they were sitting around the dying coals of the small cooking fire. Beyond them stood the wagons, the horses in a rope corral strung between the wagons.

"I was a lot more interested in saving my bacon than I was in counting noses," Longarm replied. "All I know is that I put a bullet into one of 'em, so there'll be one less jumping us."

"You're pretty sure they were sent here to attack us?" Sarah asked.

"Chances are they're heading this way right now," Longarm nodded. "Seems to me I'd be doing just what them fellows bucking Calder is aiming to, was I in their shoes."

"It would make sense," Foster agreed. "If the outfit that wants to keep Calder from going ahead gets rid of us, and then pulls up all the stakes we've set marking the right-of-way, it'd mean a new survey would have to be made. And whoever made it would be starting from scratch, just like we did."

"I'd say we've got a fight on our hands, whether we like it or not," Cross put in. He turned to Longarm and asked, "Can we hold 'em off?"

"A man would have to be a fool to make that kind of a guess," Longarm replied. "But if you want to make a stand, it'd be part of my job to fight right alongside of you."

"If you're all that sure, Long, we'd better be getting ready for them, then," O'Grady said soberly.

"Where'll we find a place to fort up?" Brown asked. "In flat country like this, there ain't a lot of places that even a little bunch like us can find to hole up in."

"How far away is the nearest broke-up country?" Longarm cut in. "You men have got all kinds of maps, I'd imagine."

"Sure we have," Foster agreed. "And after you told me about the trouble we're likely to run into I looked at the best ones. We're still three or four hours away from the closest thing you could call a canyon."

"Trouble is, them fellows might've already set out from the wash," Longarm frowned. "That's something we don't know and we got no way to find out. If we start on a three-or-four-hour move, they could trail us easy as falling off a log and catch up with us while we're on the move. If they was to do

142

that, we'd wind up between a rock and a hard place."

"That's the gospel truth," Hobbs said. "I've been out in this desert country a long time, and unless we stumble onto a deep draw big enough for all of us and the horses, too, we'd be better off forting the wagons."

Longarm said nothing for a moment. He was busy calculating the time that had elapsed earlier in the day before he ran into Foster after leaving the wash, and the time that had passed since then. His calculations were not encouraging. He glanced up at the sky. Except for a thin line of fast-fading light to the west, darkness was complete.

He said, "I been doing a little figuring. If I got it all worked out right, them fellows that come to the wash was looking for the Apache Kid and his mama to guide 'em, once they was close to us. Now, I don't imagine they'll waste a lot of time. If they figured to take us in the dark, they'd be maybe halfway here by now. We better do whatever we need to without wasting no more time jawing."

"We'll fort up behind the wagons right here then," Foster said. "It's about as good a place as any we'd find if we started moving."

For the next few minutes the impromptu camp was like an oversized beehive. Longarm and Foster moved from one wagon to another. Only the big wagon had been unhitched, and by the time Foster and the other two teams had formed a square with one side still open, Hobbs and Brown had their wagon ready to move. The square was closed quickly once Hobbs and Brown got their wagon hitched and the horses were unharnessed and led into the shelter of the improvised fort.

Once that job had been finished, the men of the survey crew began attending to their weapons. Foster started across the compact little enclosure when he saw Sarah standing pressed against the bed of the wagon she and Cross used.

"You'd better get up in the big wagon and settle down," he told her. "If Long's right and those fellows come up here to attack us, the air's going to be too full of lead for comfort."

"I'm not looking for comfort," Sarah said quickly. "Or for a safe place, either. I don't have a rifle, or even a pistol, but

143

just because I've got on a skirt, I'm certainly not going to huddle down in a wagonbed while you men do all the fighting."

"Now, Sarah——" Foster began.

Sarah interrupted him. "A bullet's a bullet, whether a man or a woman fires it," she said. "There's bound to be a spare gun I can use."

"Well, I've got a .44 Smith & Wesson in the wagon," Foster told her. "If you know how to use it——"

"I'm not too weak to pull a trigger," she broke in. "Just give me the gun. I'll use it."

Longarm had walked up in time to hear Sarah's response. He said, "You might as well give her the pistol, Foster. We'll need every shot we can get off if that outfit does jump us."

With a resigned shrug, Foster stepped over to his wagon and fumbled under the seat until he found the holstered Smith & Wesson.

"I'll just ask you to do one thing," Foster said as he handed the weapon to Sarah. "Get in the big wagon and stay in back of the water barrel. It's about the safest place you'll find."

Before he'd finished speaking, the drumming of hoofbeats sounded in the distance.

"Do like he says," Longarm told Sarah. "And don't waste no time. If I ain't wrong, you'll have a chance to use that gun inside of the next few minutes."

Chapter 15

Longarm's prediction proved to be correct, but it was wrong in its timing. For almost a quarter of an hour after the hoof-beats first shattered the night's hush, the blackness was broken only by an occasional neigh or by the thunking of hoofbeats from the area around the squared wagons. Sometimes the neighing horse was one of those inside the survey party's cramped enclosure, but more often the whinnying came from outside, when one of the attackers' mounts sensed or smelled the close presence of another of its kind.

"Damn it!" Foster grated under his breath as the minutes ticked off and the band moving around on the barren flat outside the wagons made no effort to do anything. "I wish those bastards out there'd either start shooting or go home!"

"Don't go asking for no more trouble than we already got," Longarm cautioned him. "They're in the same pickle we are, just waiting for us to start shooting and give 'em a target. I ain't saying I'd wait the way Pawley is, if he's the one in charge out there, but I sure wouldn't start nothing I wasn't sure I'd be able to finish."

"It sounds like there's a big bunch of 'em," O'Grady commented. "Maybe more'n we can handle."

"We got to handle 'em," Longarm replied.

"I guess we can cut it, but I'd feel a lot better if we had more ammunition," Hobbs put in.

Before Longarm could reply, Foster broke into the low-voiced conversation. "As long as we don't waste what we've got, we'll be all right," he said.

"Let's be glad it's the dark of the moon," Longarm said quietly. "We're a lot better off than we'd be if it was full. Just remember that they can't see to aim any better'n you can."

"I guess we'll manage to hit a few," Hobbs went on, but there was little conviction in his voice.

"You think we'll be able to hold out?" Brown asked.

"Don't look for me to say yes or no to that kind of question," Longarm replied. "I'd be a damn fool whichever I said."

"At least we've got a place to shoot from, which is more than they have," Cross reminded his companions. "All we've got to do is keep calm. With a little luck, we'll hold our own until daybreak, and then we can pick our targets."

"Daybreak's a long time away," Brown retorted.

"It'll be here sooner than you think," Longarm assured him. "And even if it wasn't nothing but a lucky fluke we even knew they was going to try and jump us, we got the edge on 'em, hunkered down the way we are."

"All the same, I'd like to have a little more edge on 'em," Brown went on.

"We got a pretty good edge now," Longarm pointed out. "We got cover, but they ain't. And we already got 'em worried, and worried men don't fight as good as ones that start into a fracas certain they're going to win."

"A little more edge wouldn't hurt my feelings," Brown said. "Just the same, I'm getting—" He broke off when a rifle shot cracked outside the wagons.

"Sounds like they're starting up," Longarm said calmly. "Now, you men remember something. Don't shoot now, but when you do, space out your shots. If you shoot two or three times real fast, them fellows out there can fix their sights on your muzzle-blast. Don't give 'em a chance to do that."

Shouts from the riders broke the night following the shot, and other shots marked by spurts of muzzle-blast stabbed the darkness as the attackers opened fire. Hot lead thunked into the stout oaken sides of the wagons, and the horsemen circling the improvised fort drew closer to their target when their fire was not answered at once.

Then the surveyors began shooting back, and when the high-pitched scream of a wounded horse cut a shrill note above the sullen reports of the attackers' rifles, a few yells rose from the wagons' defenders.

"Don't just rest your butts in your saddles, you men!" a fresh voice from the lines of the attacking horsemen called, rising above the dying spatter of rifle fire. "Get to moving, like I told you! Circle and shoot at the same time!"

"You know that voice?" Longarm asked Foster.

"No. If I ever heard it before, I don't remember it."

"I don't guess it makes much difference, at that," Longarm said. "Except it'd be sorta satisfying to know who's heading up that bunch out there."

There was another ragged volley from the horsemen, and hoofbeats began thudding on the hard ground as the attackers started circling around the squared wagons. The volume of their firing diminished as they started riding, but bullets still kept thunking into the sides of the wagons and into the baked earth beneath them.

"Hold your fire!" Longarm cautioned his companions. "Wait till they stop and bunch up again!"

While the defenders obeyed, shots from the horsemen dashing around and around outside the wagons kept cracking, red spurts of muzzle-blast breaking the darkness. Longarm listened to the scattered gunfire for several minutes, then felt his way around the little enclosure made by the wagons until he reached Foster.

"About all them fellows out there's doing is wasting a lot of powder and lead," he told the survey leader.

"That's fine, as long as they don't hit any of us," Foster replied. "The more they shoot, the sooner they'll run out."

"Don't count on it," Longarm cautioned. "I told you there

147

was a wagon with 'em when I run into 'em at the wash. I got a pretty good idea that wagon had a few cases of ammunition in it along with their grub."

"Then they've got a lot more than we have. Damn it, Longarm! We didn't come out here to fight! We just carry a box or two of shells apiece."

"That's what I been thinking," Longarm said. "And if they keep on pouring lead into us the way they're doing now, they're bound to get off a lucky shot that'll hit one of us. If you miss me for a few minutes, don't let it bother you."

"You're not going out there, I hope," Foster said.

"I ain't that big a fool, but I sorta got an idea I want to try out."

"What can I do to help?"

"Not much of anything for a minute or so. If I yell, start our fellows shooting again."

"You don't take your own advice very well, do you?" Foster asked. Longarm could not see him smiling, but there was the hint of a grin in his voice.

"My advice ain't very good sometimes," Longarm said dryly. Then he went on, "Thing is, if we keep on this way and don't do no shooting, them bastards is gonna get closer and closer and sooner or later they might get lucky. I aim to try and set 'em back a mite."

"Good luck, then," Foster told him.

Longarm leaned his Winchester against the rear wheel of the nearest wagon and sidestepped away from it to place himself between the front and back wheels. Dropping to all fours, he crawled through the open space until he was under the wagonbed. The darkness was even more dense in the confined area he now occupied than it had been before.

Reaching up, he groped along the wagonbed until he found the center shaft, a sturdy timber almost a foot square. When he raised his hand he found what he had expected he would, a clear space that provided eight or ten inches of clearance between the top of the shaft and the bottom of the wagonbed.

"It'll be a real tight fit, old son," he muttered into the darkness, "but there oughta be room for you to squeeze into."

Lying on the ground, Longarm turned on his side and slid

148

his foot between the shaft and the wagonbed. Then he levered himself up until he was stretched flat, lying facedown on the center shaft in the open area between it and the bottom of the wagonbed.

Though the spot he now occupied was confining, he managed to slide his Colt out of its holster. When he extended his arm, he found that by stretching a bit and swivelling his shoulders, the hand holding the revolver would clear the side of the wagon.

On the flat around the embattled survey party, the attacking horsemen were still circling and firing at random. Hot lead continued to thud into the sides of the wagons and to whistle through their canvas tops. The surveyors had settled down by now. Though they were letting off only one shot for every five or six fired by the attackers, they were still keeping the riders at bay.

As uncomfortable as his position was, Longarm grew accustomed to it while he bided his time. A few minutes before he had crawled under the wagon, he had noticed that he heard the voice of the man commanding the night attackers at intervals five or ten minutes apart. The voice was unmistakable. It was gravelly and harsh, and the only one that he heard regularly. Now Longarm strained to hear the voice raised again.

His vigilance was soon rewarded, though in his cramped and uncomfortable position the minutes had seemed to Longarm to drag out interminably.

"Keep moving, you men!" the commander called. "And keep giving 'em hell! These bastards can't hold out much longer!"

Longarm tensed momentarily as the voice rose above the intermittent gunfire. He stretched to the utmost as he extended the hand holding his Colt.

When the man in command shouted at his men again, Longarm was ready. Aiming only by swivelling his Colt, unable to see his target, but guided by the almost instinctive reactions that had allowed him to walk away unharmed from dozens of gunfights, Longarm used the Colt in a way that only a man with hands as large and as strong as his could handle.

His forefinger holding the trigger down, he thumbed the

hammer back and released it five times in quick succession as he swung the barrel of the weapon in a short arc. His slip-hammer firing sent one of the big .45 caliber slugs after another across a fan-shaped section of the ground in front of the wagon.

He heard a shout followed by the panicked neighing of a wounded horse. From the area his slugs had spanned, a rifle barked twice. The slugs tore into the thick sideboards of the wagon above his head. Then the voice of the outlaw leader sounded again.

"Give me a hand, Slater!" he called. "Some son of a bitch just shot shot my horse out from under me!"

Hoofbeats thudded, their dull thunking on the baked soil came close and stopped momentarily, then sounded once more. The voice of the attackers' leader rose above the intermittent gunfire again.

"Close in on 'em, men! They've got to be running short of ammunition by now!"

Responding to the command, the tempo of the attackers' firing grew faster. The darkness was broken by the red spurts of muzzle-blast as the raiders responded to their leader's command.

Longarm dropped to the ground and rolled from beneath the wagon. He holstered his Colt as he grabbed his rifle and moved to the end of the wagon. Beyond him on the flat prairie the night raiders pressed home their attack with renewed vigor.

Suddenly the form of one of the riders appeared silhoutted against the jet of brightness from the gunfire of the attacker beyond him. Longarm swung the muzzle of his rifle, snap-shotted, and saw the man who'd been his target drop his rifle and topple to the ground. The horse that found itself suddenly riderless began dashing in a wild uncontrolled zigzag as it tried to get away from the acrid smell of powder-smoke and the incessant drum of gunfire that was filling the night air.

In the little enclosure around Longarm, the men of the survey party were shouting, and some of the shouts were cries of pain. Longarm's battle-attuned ears told him that the volume of firing by the survey party was diminishing. He did not look around to confirm the message his ears were giving him. Instead, he took another sideways step. It brought him to the little gap that had been left when they formed the wagons into a square.

Though he could still see nothing except the gouts of red muzzle-blast that burst from the attackers' rifles, Longarm had a better field of fire now. He also had only half a dozen more cartridges for the Winchester left in his pocket, and he had not yet reloaded his Colt after emptying it in the quick barrage of slugs he'd fired from beneath the wagon.

"You oughta known you'd need more shells, old son," Longarm scolded himself beneath his breath as he searched the darkness for a target. "You better hold back a little bit and make every shot count, because likely everybody else is in the same fix you are."

Longarm became aware that a foreign sound was being added to the noise of the gunfight. He frowned and shook his head.

"Damned if that don't sound like there's another bunch of horses galloping up here," he muttered as scanned the gunflash-mottled blackness looking for a sure target. "But you got to be hearing things. There ain't nobody who'd be out on Frenchman Flat at this time of night."

Only a few seconds later he knew that he'd been wrong, for the drumming sound grew louder. Now he was sure his ears hadn't been deceiving him. The hoofbeats quickly drew closer and Longarm heard men shouting over the diminished noise of firing from inside the improvised fort.

Suddenly, a volley of distant shots added to the noises that were shattering the night. The firing from the raiders slackened. A second volley, ragged and not as far away, overrode the close reports of the outlaw band's rifles. Then the now-familiar voice of the nightriders' leader sounded from beyond the clustered wagons.

"Give it up, men!" the harsh voice called. "Cut a shuck for the wash! We'll have to come back later and finish the job!"

Shouts from the outlaws spread the word. The firing from

the embattled defenders of the wagon-square diminished and that from the direction of the newly arrived group began rising.

Then a voice strange to Longarm overrode the shooting, which had faded in volume as the nightriders started to retreat.

"You men go after 'em! Give 'em hell, and come back here when you got your job done!" the unseen man called.

Foster's familiar voice broke the gathering stillness. "Hold your fire, boys! That's Bart Calder out there! He's telling that new bunch what to do!"

Longarm frowned as the mixed noises of thrumming hoofbeats and scattered rifle shots began fading away.

"Foster sure don't sound like himself," he muttered under his breath in the strange new stillness of the desert night. The sounds of gunshots were distant now, the drum of galloping hoofbeats forming a minor undertone to the firing.

"Hello the wagons!" the man Foster had identified as Calder called from the flat. "This is Bart Calder, and I'm riding up to the wagons. Just don't mistake me for somebody else!"

Because of the almost constant flashes of muzzle-blast to which his eyes had been exposed during the gunfight, Longarm's eyes had been slow in adjusting again to the night's now total blackness. His night vision slowly returned, and he could see Foster standing beside his wagon. His left arm dangled limply by his side, and his right hand was clamped over his forearm.

"You taken a bullet," Longarm said as he reached Foster's side. "How bad are you hurt?"

"It could be a lot worse. The slug just nicked me a little bit. It sure stings like hell, though."

"Sarah!" Longarm called. "See if you can scare up some kind of cloth you can use for a bandage and come fix Foster's arm up."

"You better look at O'Grady first," Foster said. "He's got a bad bullet-crease in his head. Knocked him silly. He's laying in his wagon. I was going after some water for him."

A match flared inside the big wagon and a moment later

the glow of lanternlight showed through its canvas top. Sarah stuck her head out of the front flap and said, "I'll fix O'Grady before I tend to you, Jared. I guess the fighting's over now."

"It sure is," Longarm told her. "Calder and them men he brought with him didn't get here a bit too soon."

"Well, we lost a lot of time looking for you after we got over the hump from the railroad," said a husky, ruddy-faced man as he raised up after ducking into the enclosure under the bed of one of the wagons. "I had to guess at where you ought to be from the map with your survey line on it in my office."

"You'll be Bart Calder, or I miss my guess," Longarm said. He extended his hand, and while he and Calder exchanged handshakes he went on, "My name's Long, Mr. Calder. I don't guess you're surprised to see me here."

"As a matter of fact, I am," Calder replied.

He was sizing up Longarm, his brown eyes flicking in quick glances. Longarm was giving Calder the same kind of scrutiny. Calder was a tall man, almost as tall as Longarm. He had a square jaw, high ruddy cheekbones, and full lips that he kept compressed in a tight line when he was not speaking.

"We can talk about that later," he went on. "From what I heard you men saying while I was riding up, you've got some wounded to look after."

"I'm taking care of them," Sarah put in as she dropped from the wagon where O'Grady had been fighting. "Red's going to be all right. He got a bullet-crease on his head, but it's just a scalp wound."

"And who might you be?" Calder asked as she fell silent.

"Sarah Roundtree, Mr. Calder," she replied. "I don't guess the news has caught up with you yet, but I'm working for you on the survey party now."

"And doing as good a job as any man could," Foster put in quickly. "I hired Sarah on after Mose Barton got killed by the Apaches." Foster told him over Sarah's shoulder as she began bandaging the bullet-crease in his forearm.

"I'm sure you do," Calder nodded. "And I'm satisfied with the progress you've made. But it's still not fast enough, Jared. That's one reason I came down here. I've been anxious to see

153

for myself just how things are going, and see if we can't speed up. I've had some disturbing news, which is another reason for me being here. It looks like we're going to have some fights as bad as the one you men just finished before we get through building this railroad!"

Chapter 16

"But we haven't even finished the survey yet!" Foster protested.

"We'll put more men on it, then," Calder told him. "I'll find another team. They can start from the south and shoot their line up to connect with the one you're laying out."

"That'd be one way to speed up," Foster agreed.

"We'll talk about that later," Calder said. "Right now, you'd better let that young lady finish bandaging you and get a little rest."

"What about the crew?" Foster frowned. "We ought to be starting out at daybreak to push on across Frenchman Flat."

"Rest a day first," Calder told Foster. "You and your men have spent most of the night fighting, and you need time to catch up with your sleep." He turned to Sarah and went on, "I don't suppose you'd mind a little extra rest, would you?"

"Of course not," she said quickly. "And I think you're absolutely right. We'll work a lot better if we're rested."

"You see that everybody rests, then, Miss Sarah. Take that worry off Jared, and he can let his arm start healing."

By this time the sounds of Calder's men chasing the outlaws had died away completely. The night air was still except for a moan now and then from O'Grady's wagon and the low-voiced conversation between Cross, Hobbs, and Brown as they stood together in one corner of the improvised fort.

"I'll pass the word on to the others," Sarah told Calder. "But what about those men you brought with you?"

"Don't worry about them. They'll look after themselves. Now, I need to have a word or two with Marshal Long, so you go on and help Jared get his crew settled down."

"They'll be glad to rest the day out," Foster put in. "But if you need any of us—"

"Don't worry," Calder broke in. "Just do what I said." He turned to Longarm and went on, "It's time for us to have a talk. If you're not too tired, let's take a little walk out on the prairie and get acquainted."

"Well, I can't say I'm what you'd call fresh as a daisy, but I ain't too stove-in to walk a while with you," Longarm replied. "It wasn't a much of a fight, anyways. It'd've been a lot worse if we'd been jumped by Apaches."

"You won't have to worry about the Apaches, Marshal Long," Calder said. "The men I brought with me can ride herd on the redskins after they corral the gang that jumped you. And, by the way, I've got a representative of the Indian Agency coming here from Santa Fe to help get the Apaches peaceful again."

"It seems to me like you got a lot of irons in the fire," Longarm commented.

"Oh, I keep busy. A man rusts if he loafs too much."

"That's about the way I look at it," Longarm agreed.

"Things never really settle down, Long," Calder went on. "They just seem to be settled."

"I was figuring to settle down the Apaches, which is what my chief sent me here from Denver to do," Longarm went on. "But I run into Sarah. Her folks had all got killed by the same bunch of redskins that's been giving your surveyors trouble. There's a young buck that calls himself the Apache Kid leading 'em."

"They're the ones," Calder nodded. "You've run into the Apache Kid before, I understand."

"I run him down and arrested him quite a while back," Longarm nodded. "He served out his time and got released. I had another brush with him down in Vegas Wash, but it didn't play out so I could get my handcuffs on him."

"That doesn't mean you'll give up, if half of what I've heard about you is true. And that's why I asked Charlie Devens to put you on this case."

"That'd be my top boss, Attorney General Devens, back in Washington, I suppose?" Longarm asked.

"Of course," Calder nodded, as though asking a favor of a member of the United States cabinet was nothing extraordinary.

"Well, I caught up with the Apache Kid, all right. I guess you know I let him give me the slip, though."

"No, I didn't. But you've caught him twice. You'll know how to get your hands on him again."

"Unless that bunch you sent on to the Vegas Wash beats me to him. But I don't expect you care who catches him."

"Not a bit. As long as he's behind bars and can't give me any more trouble."

"Soon as I get him put away, I reckon my job's going to be finished, then," Longarm said.

"As far as I'm concerned, it is," Calder nodded. He grinned a bit ruefully and added, "And mine is just starting. I heard some news just before I left that might mean I've got something more that a few Apaches to settle down."

"But this railroad survey was at the top of your list?"

"Certainly. A lot of things depend on me getting those tracks laid down here and trains running on them."

Longarm hesitated for a moment, then asked the question that had been nagging at him since Calder and his men showed up. "I don't mind telling you, I'm real curious to find out how you knew where to find us in a place like this, Mr. Calder."

"Make it Bart, Marshal Long," Calder told him. "I don't put much stock in being formal."

"You come down to it, I don't either," Longarm nodded. "I got a sorta nickname my friends call me——"

"I've heard about it," Calder broke in. "Longarm."

157

"That's right, Bart," Longarm nodded. "But you didn't answer my question about finding just where we'd be."

"That's not any secret," Calder smiled. "In my situation, I make both friends and enemies. Major Lemuel Pawley's certainly no friend of mine, so when I heard that he was out hiring gunmen, I made it my business to find out why."

"It was Pawley and his men that jumped us, then?"

Calder nodded. "It was him, all right."

"And how'd you happen to find out about him being down here? Frenchman's Flat is a long way from Carson City."

"But Carson City's not all that far from Virginia City," Calder said. "I know a lot of people in both places. Now and then some of them look to me for a little bit of help. I always do what I can, and usually they'll do some kind of favor for me if they get a chance."

"I can see how that works," Longarm said. "And somebody you'd helped spilled the beans about that gang of outlaws getting ready to jump Jared and his outfit."

"It went a little bit deeper than that," Calder told him. "For what it's worth, Longarm, I'll give you a word of advice. If you ever have to recruit a bunch of plug-uglies to do a dirty job, and you'd like to keep me in the dark about what you're doing, don't try to find the men you need at the New Ophir Saloon in Virginia City."

"That's where Pawley went looking, was it?"

"Exactly. Now, it just happens that the man who owns the New Ophir is a good friend of mine. A few years ago I also loaned him the money to fix his place up."

Longarm nodded. "So you heard about it, I guess?"

"Within a matter of hours. That damn fool Pawley's a blabbermouth, Longarm," Calder went on. "He not only put out the word he was looking for gunhands, but mentioned where he wanted them to go."

"You don't have to go no further," Longarm said. "I've had to try and get the jump on a few like Pawley. But you sure musta hurried to catch up with him."

"I had the men I needed. I keep a few standing by all the time," Calder explained. "Getting here fast enough was the real problem. Those two railroad cars I got had to travel all over hell's half-acre. Up on the Virginia City & Truckee to connect with the SP, and then over the Sierras and down through California to that new spur they're building eastward from Barstow."

"You sorta taken the long road," Longarm suggested.

"A lot longer than I like. Luckily, Colis Huntington's also a good friend, so I didn't have any trouble getting a red-flag special for my cars all the way south through California and on that new spur they've got started across the Tehachapis. My men and I only had about an hour's horseback ride to get here."

"You sure had to do some quick moving, at that."

"I did the best I could. Even then, we didn't quite make it in time."

"I wouldn't exactly say that. You got here when it made all the difference. If it hadn't been for you and your men, we'd maybe be buzzard's meat by now."

"Well, if they have any luck, they'll get the Apaches corralled and Foster can get on with his survey," Calder said. "I want to start laying rails within the next month."

"Now, that's something I need to talk with you about, Bart," Longarm told the financier. "I ain't sure how it'll set with you, but it just might save you a lot of trouble."

"I don't know what you've got in mind, but let's put off talking any more until later. I need a couple of hours' sleep, and I'm sure you do, too. The chuck wagon ought to be here by the time we wake up, and I'll feel more like talking after I've had some rest and a bite of breakfast."

Longarm didn't try to hide his astonishment. His jaw dropped, he stared at Calder for a moment, then he asked, "You got a chuck wagon along with that outfit you brought?"

"Why, certainly. I knew Foster and his crew weren't likely to be carrying enough grub for the bunch I had with me, and I'm damned if I'll ask my men to fight or work with empty bellies."

"I've got to give you credit, Bart. You sure do travel first-class," Longarm grinned. "But I could handle a little shut-eye myself, so whatever you say's all right with me."

• • •

By the time Longarm and Calder found a chance to talk again, the climbing sun was high in the sky and the morning air was beginning to grow warm. The dying breeze spread the tempting aroma of frying bacon from the fly the chuck wagon crew had erected after they'd finally reached the survey party's camp.

On one side of the chuck wagon, Foster and his crew had lined up their wagons after breaking the defensive square in which they'd forted up to fight off their attackers. The dozen men Calder had brought with him had made their own camp after returning from the Vegas Wash. Their report was encouraging. By the time they'd reached the cavern, the raiding party had left.

"I didn't figure you'd want us to take after 'em," the leader told Calder. "We gave 'em a pretty good walloping when we got here, so they won't be apt to come back and try again."

"I imagine they're cutting a shuck all the way back north," Calder nodded. "But this place here is home to the Apaches, so they might make another try to stop us. You and your boys might do a little scouting around after breakfast, though, just in case they're lurking close by and getting ready to attack again. We'll stick around until the fellow from the Indian Agency shows up. Then we'll leave it up to him to set things straight."

Longarm had been listening while Calder and his posse leader talked. He waited until the other man left, then said, "You know, Bart, what you and him was talking about puts me in mind of what I started telling you last night."

"Maybe you'd better tell me now, then," Calder suggested.

"Well, I hate to bust into something that ain't rightly my business," Longarm began, "but I got an idea that might save you a lot of trouble down the line."

"If that's the case, I'm interested. Trouble costs money and takes time that I could be using doing something better than straightening out problems. Go ahead, tell me your idea."

"It's about this railroad you're building, Bart. Why'd you pick out Frenchman Flat to run your rails through? From what I seen of mining in these parts, the flats don't run to much ore."

160

"Certainly not. Just about all the mineral deposits worth working are in the mountains on both sides of the flats."

"Then why're you pushing rails right across the middle?" Longarm persisted.

"Why, the civil engineers I hired used these newfangled French slide rules to show me that it'll cost less to lay the rails in a straight line across this flat country and use wagons to haul the ore to the railroad than it would to curve the rails around the flat along the foothills close to the mines."

"I oughta known it was something like that," Longarm nodded. Then he asked, "I don't guess them slide rules knows a lot about Indians, do they?"

Calder frowned for a moment before saying, "I'm not sure I follow you."

"Well, I reckon what I'm trying to say is that just about all the figuring men I ever run into puts more store in their figures than they do in the way folks acts. That's why I asked you if there ain't a better place to run them tracks than right through the middle of Frenchman Flat."

"If there is, I don't know about it. The rails can be laid almost in a straight line from north to south, and everybody knows a straight line's the shortest way to travel."

"Sure, I understand that," Longarm nodded. "But short ain't going to save you no time if you got to stop and fight every day or so to keep them rails pushing ahead."

"That needs a little explanation," Calder frowned. "Are you saying that the Indians are going to keep attacking my crews, even after the rails are laid?"

"It wouldn't surprise me none. Frenchman Flat is is about the only place that's left where the big herds of wild horses has got room to bunch up."

"What's that got to do with my railroad?"

"Maybe not much, maybe a pretty big lot," Longarm went on. "Right now, just about all the redskins from Nevada and Arizona Territory and New Mexico comes here to catch their horses. They ain't going to like it a bit when your railroad runs off them wild horse herds."

"If the wild horse herds move, the Indians will follow them," Calder said. "They won't have much choice."

161

"Maybe not. But don't you figure they'll get mad and take out their mad on your trains?"

"If they do, I'll put sharpshooters on the ore trains."

"What if the redskins just keep on tearing up your tracks?" Longarm asked.

Calder was silent for a moment, a thoughtful frown growing on his face. The thoughtfulness in his features was reflected in his voice when he replied to Longarm's question.

"Now, that might be another matter. If they did that, they'd slow everything down. Slowdowns of that kind might be so expensive that neither the mines or the railroad would pay their way. And if I had to keep a small army of men down here to fight off the Indians, that'd run up my expenses, too."

"Well, it sure ain't my place to tell you what to do, Bart," Longarm said. "You'd know a lot better'n me what's best."

"Right this minute, I'm not sure I do. You're suggesting that it'd cost more to keep fighting off the Indians than it would to circle the rails around the flat and be sure the trains would be able to run on schedule."

"That's about it," Longarm agreed.

"That's something I'll have to think about. I'm already out of pocket for the survey Foster and his crew are making, and they're close to winding up the job. I'd hate to have it all to do over again."

"It'd be a lot cheaper if whoever hired Pawley and his plug-uglies don't stir up no more trouble," Longarm suggested. "And if the Indians don't jump your ore trains or tear up the tracks."

His brow furrowing, Calder said thoughtfully, "I can find out who was behind Pawley and handle him. But I'll appreciate it if you forget you heard me say so."

"What you do is your business, of course," Longarm said quickly.

"It's not any secret that I've got a few business enemies," Calder went on. "But I'll take care of them in my own time and in my own way, just as I always have."

"I ain't aiming to ask no questions about who sent Pawley after you. That's private between you and him."

"Now, the Apaches are a different thing," Calder went on.

"Even the government can't handle them all the time, or General Miles wouldn't be down in Arizona Territory chasing Geronimo. But say you take the Apache Kid back to prison—how long will he have to serve?"

"I don't recall how much time he's got left. He wasn't pardoned, just paroled, so chances are he won't get put away very long. And Apache Annie won't be locked up long, either. All she can get sent up for is interfering with a U.S. marshal, and that ain't going to keep her behind bars very long."

Calder nodded. "I won't argue about that. Well, you've given me a lot to think about, Longarm. If I can get those two out of Nevada long enough to finish laying track, and if I can see that circling Frenchman Flat with my railroad instead of cutting across it will save me as much time and trouble as you seem to think it will, I've got a hunch I'll change my plans."

"It looks like all we got to do is wait for that fellow from the Indian Agency to show up, then," Longarm said. "Soon as he gets here, I'll be going with him after Annie and the Apache Kid. They'll be outa the way of your survey crew in just a few days at most."

Longarm was stretched out on a makeshift pallet in the big wagon, catching up with the sleep he'd lost during the past few nights, when Sarah Roundtree lifted the back cover-flap and called to him.

"I hate to break up your nap," she said. "But there's a buggy coming this way across the flat, and Bart thinks it might be the man you're waiting for from the Indian Bureau."

"I'll be right along soon as I step into my boots," he replied. Reaching for his footgear, he went on, "I'm sorry I been so busy, Sarah. It seems like I ain't had time to set down and talk with you for a minute lately. But I don't guess you'd've had much time to spare, either."

"I've been just about as busy as you have," she said. "But at least I haven't had a lot of extra cooking to do, thanks to that kitchen outfit and the cook Bart brought along. You know, he's really a very nice man, Longarm."

"You mean the cook?"

"Don't be silly! I mean Bart Calder!" She frowned. "Is he really as rich as they say he is?"

"I don't figure he needs to worry about where his next bowl of beans is coming from. But he's all right. I got to put in with you on that."

"He might be rich," Sarah went on, "but it sure hasn't spoiled him or made him stuck-up."

"And on top of that, he pulled our bacon outa the fire just when it was starting to get burnt," Longarm said as he made his way to the tailgate and dropped to the ground. "You know, the way you talk about him, I got a hunch you sorta like him."

"Well, I do, but that's all."

They walked in silence past the line of wagons. Longarm saw the buggy that was drawing steadily closer across the flat. It was within a quarter of a mile of the wagons now, etched sharply by the bright sunlight against the green of the sage.

"I guess you'll be going out with the Indian Agency man as soon as he gets here, won't you?" Sarah asked.

"Soon as I can," Longarm nodded. He pulled a cigar from his pocket and lighted it before adding, "I got to chase after the Apache Kid and his mama before their trail gets cold."

"And you don't know whether or not you'll be back before we start the survey again?"

"That's going to depend on what Bart decides to do about going on with it."

Longarm spoke abstractedly, his eyes on the buggy. It was very close now, but the brilliant sunshine behind it shaded its interior. Though he strained his eyes, he could not see the driver. He and Sarah were still gazing at the buggy, sun-blinded, when it pulled to a stop in front of them. Longarm gasped and almost dropped the cigar from his mouth when the driver stood up. He glanced into the buggy, but saw no other passenger. Then he turned to Sarah.

"Maybe you better be the first one to say hello," he whispered. "The last thing I'd've thought about the Indian Bureau doing was to send a woman out on this job, but that's just what they've gone and done!"

Chapter 17

"Longarm, I can't talk for Bart! I just work on one of his survey crews!" Sarah protested, speaking in a whisper. "What on earth could I say to her?"

"All you got to do is tell her what you just said, that you work for Bart and you'll show her where he is."

Before Sarah could speak, the newcomer solved the problem for both her and Longarm by saying, "I am Ynez Roybal. I have come here from Santa Fe to represent the United States Indian Agency, and I am looking for a man named Calder."

"I'll be glad to show you where to find him," Sarah said quickly. "I know he's been expecting you."

"Very good," the newcomer replied. "If you would like to ride with me in the buggy—"

"Go on, Sarah," Longarm told her. "I'll walk over." As Sarah moved to the buggy and got in he went on, "If you're wondering why I butted in, Miz Roybal, my name's Custis Long, and you and me work for the same boss. I'm a deputy United States marshal."

Longarm's words must have registered on the Indian

165

Agency representative, but her face still showed no expression as she replied in response to his introduction, "I hope you have not arrested any of our people, Marshal. I have been told there is trouble here."

"I ain't arrested nobody yet, but I reckon I'll have to before this ruckus is settled," Longarm told her. "You see, Miz Roybal, them Apaches you call 'your people' has been giving the folks that work on the railroad a real bad time. Come right down to it, I got crossways of some of 'em, too. And Sarah can tell you about how 'your people' murdered her aunt and uncle just a little while ago, out on the prairie."

While he talked, Longarm was studying the newcomer. Ynez Roybal had the thin high-bridged nose and arched nostrils of a Spanish aristocrat. Twin strands of jet-black hair looped down below her hat to cover her ears. Her cheekbones were high, her jawline sharp and narrow. Her lips were unusually full, and deep red. Longarm could tell nothing of her figure, for in spite of the day's warmth she had on a caped traveling cloak that concealed her body in its voluminous folds.

"You saw this happen, this murder you claim took place?" she asked.

Longarm held his temper in check and replied levelly, "I didn't see no actual killing, but I buried what was left of Sarah's kinfolks' bodies. I taken 'em out of the wagon them savages you call 'your people' had set fire to and dug their graves and covered 'em up. Is that close enough to seeing 'em killed to suit you?"

"Marshal Long didn't tell you anything but the facts, Miss Roybal," Sarah said quickly. "And I did see my aunt and uncle killed by a band of painted savages that shot them and set fire to their wagon. I barely escaped myself."

"Let us postpone discussion until later," the Indian agent said. "And if you do not mind, I prefer to be addressed as *Señorita* Roybal rather than 'Miss.' Now, if you find it convenient, I would like to talk to this *Señor* Calder I have made such a long and uncomfortable journey to meet."

Sarah pointed to the canvas fly over the cooking area. "Just pull your buggy past the wagons to that canopy," she said. Her voice was as expressionless as Ynez Roybal's had been. "And I'll find Mr. Calder for you."

You're gonna have a real job on your hand with this Roybal woman, old son, Longarm told himself as he followed the wagon to the canopy. *She's the kind that acts like they sweetens their coffee with prussic acid. Or maybe she drinks acid straight instead of coffee. If she's the kind that the Indian Agency's hiring now, it ain't no wonder the redskins keeps cutting up.*

Sarah and Ynez Roybal had alighted from the buggy and were standing in the shade of the fly by the time Longarm walked up to them. The big Sibley stove that stood in its center was cold, and the planks that outlined the dining area were bare. Sarah's lips, compressed into a thin angry line, showed Longarm her disapproval of the visitor.

"If you'll keep *Miss* Roybal company for a minute or two, I'll go see if I can find Bart," she told Longarm. "He's the one who sent for her, so it's going to be up to him to explain things. Who knows, she might even listen to him."

Without waiting for Longarm's reply, she flounced off, her chin tilted and her back stiff. Longarm turned to Ynez Roybal.

"Sorry there ain't no chairs," he said. "But I guess you can set on the counter if you've a mind to, or get back in your buggy."

"I prefer to stand," she replied. "I have been sitting in the buggy for two days, since leaving the train."

"Now, I ain't meaning to criticize the folks you work for, Miz Roybal," he said. "But I been wondering why your boss at the Agency didn't send a man along with you, to sorta help you on the trail, and all like that."

"I need no help, Marshal," she answered. "And the man you refer to as my boss at the Agency is my father. He did not send me, and I refused his offer to send someone with me. I volunteered to come here because I speak the Apache tongue fluently. It will be of great help when I talk with them."

"I'm afraid the Apaches in these parts ain't the talking kind," Longarm told her. "Now, I wouldn't advise—"

"You will pardon me for being very frank, Marshal," she broke in. "I did not solicit your advice. I will investigate and make my own decisions."

Before Longarm could reply, Barton Calder came up to the pair. His face was sober. He looked at Ynez Roybal and his eyebrows rose. Then he said, "I'm Calder, Miss Roybal. The one who's trying to build a railroad, if you can get the Indians off my back. Ever since they started laying out my right-of-way across Frenchman Flat, the Apaches have been giving us trouble."

"I don't particularly care for your choice of words, Mr. Calder," Ynez Roybal said, her voice icy. "If you are trying to build a railroad across the Apache's territory, you cannot blame them for protecting their lands from invasion."

"Frenchman Flat's not Apache land," Calder replied. "There are four Indian reservations in Nevada, in case you don't already know it. One's just a little ways north of here at Walker Lake, there's one up above it at Pyramid Lake, another one on the Idaho line up north, and the other one's over to the east, along the Utah border."

"I'm aware of their locations," she replied. "I studied the Agency's maps before I started here from Santa Fe."

"Then you know my railroad's not close to any one of them," Calder told her.

"I also know that your railroad is crossing the area where the Indians must come to capture wild horses," the Indian agent replied. "According to the documents I looked at in the Agency office, Frenchman Flat has always been common ground for the Indians. Even the tribes which are not friendly with each other do not fight when they come here to capture horses."

Longarm had been listening with growing impatience to the sparring between Calder and Ynez Roybal. Now he decided to break in and try to get them to consider the realities of the matter.

"It ain't rightly my business," he said, "but if the redskins can get along with each other while they're chasing horses here on Frenchman Falt, it looks to me like it's the Indian Agency's job to tell 'em they got to get along with Bart's

168

railroad while it's being built and after the trains start running."

"That is what I have in mind to arrange," Ynez Roybal said. "On my way to Nevada, I worked out a plan."

"Well, that sounds good," Calder said. "Suppose you tell me about it."

"I will visit each of the tribes in turn," she went on. "I will get them to agree to leave the railroad alone. In return, Mr. Calder, I will ask you to agree that your men will not harass the Indians when they come here for their horse-catching."

Shaking his head, Calder said, "I'm afraid it won't be that simple, Miss Roybal. You might get the peaceful tribes like the Chemihuevis and the Diggers to hold off harassing us, but the Apaches are another story. There's more than one Apache like the Kid and his mother that keep 'em all stirred up."

"Then I must talk to them," she said. "I'm sure that I can get them to agree not to stir up trouble."

"You'll have to find 'em before you can do that," Longarm put in. "I'm after the Apache Kid myself. He got out on parole from the federal pen and then broke his parole by getting mixed up in this fracas between the Apaches and the railroad. Now I got to take him back to serve out his term."

"And the Kid's mother?" she asked. "I believe you call her Apache Annie."

"You been doing your homework, Miz Roybal," Longarm nodded. "They're the pair I'm after. Annie's going to have to serve a little time, too. She joined up with the Kid in—well, the pair of 'em was about ready to get rid of me, so Annie's going to stand trial for interfering with a federal officer when he was trying to do his duty. And both of 'em was mixed up with the bunch of plug-uglies that jumped Bart's survey crew."

"Apparently you've either been careless, or at least something less than diligent, Marshal Long," Ynez Roybal said icily. "I sent a telegram to your superiors in Denver before leaving Santa Fe. They sent me the bare details of your assignment, but the message said nothing about this woman you call Apachie Annie, or your authority to interfere with Mr. Calder's survey workers."

"Now, don't go any further before you hear the facts, Miss

169

Roybal!" Bart Calder broke in. "I asked the Justice Department in Washington to send Longarm here to arrest the Apache Kid, just as I asked the Indian Agency to have a representative come help me clear up the trouble that the Apaches have been giving my surveyors."

"I'm aware of your political influence, Mr. Calder," she said stiffly. "But it doesn't impress me. You see, my family has some small influence in New Mexico, so I understand how the political process works."

"Politics don't enter into it!" Calder snapped. "I'm trying to get a railroad built here, but the Indians keep trying to stop me. Longarm's not interfering with my surveyors. He's doing his part of the job, so why don't you get busy and do yours?"

"I fully intend to, Mr. Calder. I have maps in the buggy. If you will mark them so that I can find the Apaches, I'll start at once and tell them that they must leave your surveyors and your railroad alone, when it's built."

Longarm and Calder exchanged glances. Neither man spoke for a moment. Then Longarm said, "If I knew where the Apaches was, I'd be glad to mark a map for you, Miz Roybal. But I don't. I can't do no more than tell you where there's a cave that the Kid and Apache Annie uses for a hide-out. Maybe you'll find 'em there and maybe you won't, but it's the most I can do."

"That will be quite satisfactory," Ynez Roybal nodded. She started for the buggy, saying over her shoulder, "I'll get my map."

As Ynez started for her buggy, Calder said under his breath to Longarm, "I can't believe the Indian Agency would send somebody like that to try and settle this thing with the Apaches!"

"They did," Longarm pointed out.

"I can see right now that I've made a bad mistake," Calder went on. "I ought've known better, the Indian Agency being what it is. But I still feel responsible for her. Can't you give me a hand here, Longarm?"

"You don't even have to ask, Bart," Longarm replied. "I feel just about like you do. She ain't what I'd call helpless, or she never would've got here to begin with. The trouble is, she's too used to them Indians in New Mexico. They're mostly friendly, and them *pueblos* they live in is just about like towns. She don't know what she's getting into."

"I'll agree with everything you've said, Longarm, but that doesn't solve the problem."

"Well, now," Longarm went on, "I don't see as there's any way we can stop her, but I figure to follow her and see that she don't get into no real bad trouble."

"I was hoping you'd say that," Calder said, exhaling a big sigh of relief. "But I didn't feel like asking you outright."

"I'll give her a pretty good start," Longarm told Calder. "She won't be able to get much of a look in back of her in that buggy, and I can keep an eye on her without her ever knowing I'm around. But if I don't get back with her by tomorrow night, you might send a couple of your fellows out to trail us."

"I'll be glad to," Calder nodded. "In fact, I'll—" He broke off as Ynez Roybal returned carrying a roll of paper.

"Now, if you'll just show me where I can find the Apaches," she said, unrolling the map, "I'll get started and see if I can't straighten things out."

Longarm looked at the map. He put his hornlike forefinger on it just east of the center of the Spring Mountains and said, "We're right about here. Now, there ain't no landmarks to guide by here on Frenchman Flat. You just ride north and a little bit east till you hit a big gully. That'll be the Vegas Wash. Go on down the wash a ways. It'll keep widening up as you go on. Pretty soon you'll run across a little spring dripping outa the wall. That cave Apache Annie and her boy uses is on the left-hand side just a ways past the spring. There ain't no way you can miss it."

If Longarm had expected thanks for the information he'd given, he would have been disappointed. Ynez Roybal merely nodded and said casually, "I'm sure I'll find it. And I hope I can be back here by this time tomorrow."

Longarm and Calder watched her get into the buggy and gee up the horse. Neither of them spoke until the buggy's top had shrunk to a small black hump on the horizon. Then Longarm said, "I guess I better start now, Bart. I don't want to trail her too close, but I ain't aiming to let her get outa eyeball range, either."

"Good luck," Calder told him. "And I hope you don't need it."

His livery horse was still standing waiting, its reins looped over the rope corral. Longarm walked over to the animal, straightened the reins, and swung into the saddle. With a wave to Calder, he set out to follow the buggy across Frenchman Flat.

You got to give credit where it's due, old son, Longarm told himself as Ynez Roybal's buggy dipped down the slope and headed for the mouth of Vegas Wash. *She kept moving straight as a string and went right to the place she was looking for.*

Ahead of him, the buggy was vanishing down the sloping floor of the wide chasm. Remembering how the wash began curving a short distance after it was entered from from the flat, Longarm touched his pony's flank with his boot toe. The stocky dapple speeded up, but the buggy was already out of sight when the hard thunking of its hooves faded as it stepped off the baked earth of the flat and onto the thick layer of loose white sand that formed the floor of Vegas Wash.

Now, with the thunking of his mount's hoofbeats on hard-baked soil no longer a problem, Longarm prodded his mount to a faster walk. He touched the reins to slow it down again when his ears caught the thin echo of creaking harness and the almost inaudible squeak of wheels compressing the sandy bottom. A score or so yards later, he recognized the spot he was passing by the dark blotches of blood that still crusted the snow-white sand. It was the area where he'd confronted Haven and Dorsey.

Though the spots where hooves and boots had disturbed the floor of the wash had been obliterated by horses passing over them, the bloodstais were still visible. His examination of the blotched floor of the wash had diverted Longarm's attention. He suddenly glimpsed the buggy ahead and twitched the reins to slow his horse down until he could no longer see the moving vehicle. After that he was careful not to move too fast.

Secure in the knowledge that there was no way for the buggy to leave the canyon until it had passed the mouth of the cave and reached the breached spot in the canyon wall, he moved steadily forward.

Now, however, Longarm was a bit more cautious. He kept just close enough to the buggy to hear the muffled thuds of the horse's hooves on the sand and the occasional faint creaking sounds that came from the buggy. He was ready to rein in when Ynez Roybal's voice broke the silence.

"Parase!" she said. Her voice was raised only slightly, but in the silence it sounded very loud. The thunking hoofbeats of the horse stopped. There were a few more squeaks from the buggy, then only silence.

Longarm looked around. There was such a sameness about the walls and floor of the widening canyon that he could not tell for a moment where he was in relation to the cave. Then he heard faint splashes ahead and realized that the buggy must have stopped beside the spring. He sat motionless for a few moments, expecting to hear the buggy begin moving again, but as time passed and he still heard nothing but the continuing tinkle of water splashing he swung noiselessly from his saddle and crept forward.

As he advanced, the tinkling of water sounded louder. Moving slowly, his boots making no sound on the soft yielding sand, he crept toward the spring, hugging the almost vertical wall. Then he caught sight of Ynez Roybal standing beside the trickle of water that cascaded down the canyon's side.

She was beside the spring, bending forward. She'd taken off her hat and unbound her hair. Her cloak and blouse made a heap on the snow-white sand out of reach of the splashing water. Naked to the waist, her hands were busy splashing water from the little stream that trickled down the wall. As she leaned forward, the twin globes of her full breasts bobbed slowly, their dark pink tips pebbled by the cool water dripping from them.

Longarm suppressed the gasp of surprise that rose almost involuntarily from his throat. He watched as the object of his unexpected admiration cupped water in her hands and let it

173

stream from her shoulders as she ran her palms along her shoulders and throat, then down the pair of luscious pebbled globes to her waist. He noticed then that she'd tucked a towel into the waistband of her skirt. She pulled it free and began to dry herself.

With each movement she made, her bulging breasts swayed involuntarily. Longarm felt the beginning of an erection. Then, suddenly embarrassed by the peeping-Tom role he was playing, he took a backward step and walked back to his horse, placing his feet carefully to avoid any crunching sound that might give away his presence. He started to take out one of his diminishing supply of cigars, but thought better of it.

Old son, he mused, *that's a mighty pretty girl up there ahead, even if she's got some damn plaguing ways. But she ain't for you, so you just better wipe away what you seen and go about your business whenever you're around her.*

A scream from the direction of the spring broke Longarm's train of thought off short. Drawing his Colt as he moved, he started toward the spring at a run. When he rounded the curved canyon wall, he stopped as quickly as he had started.

Standing only a yard from Ynez Roybal he saw the Apache Kid, a rifle leveled at her. The Kid was not watching the woman, though. He had his fathomless obsidian eyes fixed on Longarm.

"I was sure you'd come running when the woman yelled," the Apache Kid said. His voice was as menacing as the rumble of a clap of thunder from a low-hanging raincloud. He went on, "I seen you when you was peeking at the girl. Didn't know you'd be coming back so soon, Longarm. But now you're here, you might as well get ready to stay. Yessir. You're going to stay here the rest of your life. But don't worry. That won't be very long."

Chapter 18

Longarm was not foolhardy. Staring down the muzzle of a gun held by an enemy always stirred his anger, but not to the point of making the kind of senseless move that would end his life.

"Seems to me we been over this before, and not too long ago, either," he told the Apache Kid calmly. "You didn't put me away then, and I don't figure you're man enough to do it now."

"Shut up!" the Kid snapped. "Last time you waited till I was gone, and you got away from Annie. This time I'll be keeping my eye on you as long as I let you stay alive, which ain't going to be very long."

Ynez Roybal spoke suddenly, a string of guttural grunts and rising-inflected syllables which Longarm recognized as belonging to the Apache language. It was one of several Indian tongues which he did not speak. He could catch only an occasional simple word of what the Indian Agency woman was saying.

When she finished speaking, the Apache Kid answered her. He also spoke in Apache. When he fell silent, she turned to Longarm and said, "He tells me you are his blood enemy and that because you have brought me here, I must die with you! Marshal Long, this man says he's going to kill me!"

"If that's what he said, you can just bet that's what he aims to do," Longarm replied calmly.

"But you did not bring me here! You followed me! I did not know you would do that! And I have done nothing to harm this man or his tribe!" she protested.

"If I ain't wrong, it was one of the old Apache chiefs that said something about his enemies' friends being his enemies, too," Longarm told her. "And even if we wasn't traveling together, the Kid thinks we was. That's all he needs."

"But I am not his enemy! I came to help him!"

"Now, I ain't one to point fingers, but when you pulled up at the survey camp, I tried to tell you the Kid was a bad one, and you wasn't one bit interested in listening to me."

"But he can't just kill us in cold blood!" she protested. "That's not the way our people do things today. Even the Apaches are peaceful!"

"That's as may be," Longarm told her. His voice was still level and unworried. "And I reckon a lot of Apaches is, but this one here sure ain't."

"Both of you shut up!" the Kid commanded, his voice harsh. "You—" He jerked his head at Ynez Roybal without taking his eyes off Longarm. "Hurry and dress!"

Then he spoke again in Apache, and her eyes grew wide as she listened to the short syllables. From the occasional word Longarm understood, he could only guess what the Apache Kid was saying, but when the Kid fell silent Ynez Roybal did not reply. She picked up her clothing from the ground and began putting it on. While she was busy, the Kid kept his eyes fixed on Longarm, the barrel of his rifle unwavering.

Longarm debated briefly, then decided he would try to keep the Apache Kid talking in spite of the threats he'd made. He'd learned that a man who held another at gunpoint was generally quicker to shoot during the first few instants of the confrontation than he would be later, after a few words had been exchanged between the two. It was a gamble at best, but he decided he had more to gain than to lose.

"How come you and Annie's still around here?" he asked. "I sorta figured you'd hightail it out when them outlaws that was helping you turned and run."

"They do not fight like we of the Apacheria!" the Kid said angrily. "They are like all you white men! Cowards! They have gone back where they came from. Now I will waste no more words with you!" He turned to Ynez and went on, "Hurry!"

Though he did not like the Apache Kid's increasing edginess, Longarm decided to persist. He went on, still speaking calmly, "You know, Kid, you oughta be thanking me instead of saying you're going to shoot me. If it hadn't been for me, you never would've got your hands on this lady you're looking at now."

"I told you to keep quiet, Longarm!" the Kid snapped. "If you open your mouth again, I'll kill you right here and now!"

This time Longarm did not reply, but Ynez looked up from the buttons of the blouse she had been fastening and said, "Please don't be foolish, Marshal Long! I think he means it!"

"Oh, I don't doubt for a minute that he does," Longarm told her. "But I don't expect he wants to shoot me. That'd be too easy. The Kid wants to hurt me a lot first."

"You're damned right I do!" the Apache grated. "I owe you too much misery to let you die quick and easy! And Annie owes you a few things, too. She'll enjoy helping me."

Dropping back into Apache, Ynez spoke to the Kid. He let her talk for a moment before stepping to her side and slapping her across the mouth with the back of his hand.

Longarm saw his chance and flexed his arm to draw. Before he could get his hand in motion, the Kid shifted the muzzle of his rifle the fraction of an inch needed to bring it to bear on Longarm's chest again.

"I wanta save you for me and Annie to carve on a while," he gritted. "But that ain't going to stop me from dropping you right here and now if I have to!"

Ynez started to speak, but the Apache Kid cut her short with another burst of Apache gutturals. When she stared at him and again opened her mouth to speak, he slapped her for the second time. This blow was harder than the first one. A trickle of blood started flowing from her mouth and ran down her chin. Staring at the Kid, she did not try to say anything more, but brought her hand up to her mouth to stop the flow of blood.

"I guess you see I mean what I been telling you," the Apache Kid told her. "So maybe now you'll move a little faster when I tell you to do something."

"What is it you want me to do?"

"Step over by Longarm and take his gun out of his holster and hand it to me. Don't get no smart ideas, neither. You understand?"

When Ynez dropped her hand from her mouth to reply, the blood started trickling from her cut lip again. She flinched as the first drops ran down her already bloody chin, choked and coughed, then quickly covered her mouth with her hand again. Her eyes fixed on the Apache Kid, she nodded.

"You don't need to say anything," the Kid said. "Just take Longarm's gun. And you do it the way I tell you to. Lift it out of his holster and take hold of it by the barrel, then hand it to me butt first. You understand what I said?"

This time she did not try to answer, but only nodded. The Kid gestured with the muzzle of his rifle. Ynez stepped over to Longarm's side and lifted his Colt out of its holster. Obeying the Kid's instructions, she reversed the big pistol gingerly and extended the butt to the Apache.

As the Kid moved closer to Ynez to reach for the pistol, he kept the muzzle of his rifle leveled at Longarm's midsection. Longarm was careful to stand stock-still during the few moments while the weapon was being transferred. The Kid shoved the pistol into his belt and stepped back.

"Now then," he said "we're going down to the cave where Annie is. I haven't got anything to tie you up with, but that don't matter any more. I'm the one that's got all the guns, and I'll cut either one of you down in a minute if you don't do like I tell you to."

"You don't need to worry, Kid," Longarm said calmly. "We got too much sense to cross you as long as you keep holding that rifle on us."

178

"Move, then," the Apache Kid commanded. "Longarm, let the woman step around in front of you and go first. I don't want her getting between you and me."

Longarm and Ynez began moving to obey the Kid's orders. As they came close together, Longarm managed to whisper to her.

"Do what he says," he warned. "And don't worry. Nothing bad's gonna happen for a while."

With the Apache Kid behind them, they started walking down the wash. Their slow walk to the mouth of the cavern took only a few minutes. In front of the black yawning mouth of the underground hideout, the Kid commanded them to stop.

"Annie!" he called. "I got some prisoners out here you'll be glad to see! Bring something to tie 'em up with!"

Apache Annie came out of the cave in a moment. She was wearing the same calico skirt she'd had on the last time Longarm had seen her. She carried a handful of rawhide strips, and Longarm was sure he recognized them, too.

"Damned if it ain't Longarm hisself!" she said, her thick lips splitting into a wide grin. "And who in hell's this girl with him?"

"She says she's from the Indian Agency and she come here to help us," the Kid replied. "But being as she was with Longarm, I say she's a damned liar."

"We can find out the truth of it from her real quick," Annie grinned. "I ain't forgot the ways that'll make 'em talk."

"You do not need to torture me," Ynez said. "I have told the truth. Let me go to my buggy. I have papers there that will prove I do not lie!"

"Well, what d'you say, boy?" Apache Annie asked.

"I say we better get 'em inside and go to work on 'em," the Kid replied. "Maybe I'll take a turn at the girl first. But Longarm's the one I want to work on. He's got a lot coming to him for what he did to me."

"There ain't much use tying their hands out here, then," Annie said. "I'll wait till we get 'em inside and tie their hands and feet at the same time."

She was turning to go back into the cave as she spoke.

179

Ynez turned her head to look questioningly at Longarm.

"Go on, follow Annie," he told her. "We ain't got much to say about it."

"Damned right, you haven't," the Kid snarled as he watched Ynez start with Annie into the short arced passageway that led into the cavern. "You get moving too!"

Longarm took his time turning to start for the mouth of the passageway cavern that yawned only a step or two ahead. He held his breath for a moment, wondering if the Apache Kid was taut enough to trigger the rifle. He released the breath in a silent sigh of relief when he felt the gun's muzzle dig painfully into his back and give him the chance he'd been gambling that his move would offer him.

Lurching suddenly backward and turning sharply in the same split-second, Longarm pulled his derringer from his lower vest pocket. He twirled and brought up his left arm to push the rifle barrel aside as he completed his turn. The Apache Kid triggered the rifle a fraction of a second too late.

Longarm felt a rush of warm air across his back as the bullet ripped harmlessly through the fabric of his vest and spatted angrily against the wall. He completed his turn, bringing up the derringer's muzzle as he moved.

When Longarm triggered the derringer, only inches separated it from the Apache Kid's chest. The short slug from the stubby little derringer slammed into the Kid and knocked him backward as it plowed through his chest into his heart. The Apache Kid toppled slowly. The rifle dropped from his hands and thudded into the soft sand as his body crumpled and he fell beside it.

Longarm let himself fall, too. He kept his right hand clenched around the derringer's curved butt. Annie came into the cave-mouth at a run. A long knife gleamed in her hand. She saw Longarm lying on the ground beside the motionless, bleeding body of her son. The wild scream that burst from her throat was one more of anger and vengeance than of sorrow.

Leveling the knife, she started toward Longarm. He always fought shy of shooting women, but this time he had no choice. He waited until Apache Annie was almost on him, the distance too short for the derringer's slug to miss. Its muzzle was only inches away from her knife hand when Longarm squeezed the trigger to let off the little double-barrelled weapon's second shot.

Annie did not cry out when the soft lead of the big bullet spatted into her arm and the knife dropped to the floor of the cavern. Ignoring her wound, she dived for Longarm, the fingers of her unwounded hand curved into talons. Longarm grabbed Annie's wrist before her clawed fingers reached his face. He twisted sharply and Annie fell heavily on the sandy floor beside him.

Ynez Roybal darted in, following Annie. She grasped the Apache woman's wounded arm and grabbed it to stop the jetting blood. The pain Annie felt was registered in the yowling scream that burst from her throat and died away as her eyelids fluttered and her voice faded to silence as she lost consciousness.

"We must quickly put a tourniquet on her arm," Ynez said, "or she will bleed to death."

"Sure," Longarm agreed as he got to his feet. He picked up the knife Annie had dropped and was bending to rip a strip of cloth from the bottom of Annie's dress when he saw one of the long leather thongs Annie had been carrying dangling from Ynez's wrist. He cut off the strip of supple leather, looped it quickly into a knot, and used the handle of the knife to twist the loop until it bit into Annie's arm and its pressure stopped the jets of blood.

"Damned if you can't get into more trouble than any man I ever saw!" Barton Calder said from the mouth of the cave. "It looks like you've been having some trouble. I figured you might, so I decided to follow you and see if I could help."

"Well, now," Longarm replied as he rose to his feet, "that was real thoughtful, Bart, but you got here a mite too late."

"So I see," Calder nodded. He looked at Ynez Roybal, who was standing staring at Annie's unconscious form and the sprawled body of the Apache Kid. Calder went on, "How about you, Miss Roybal?"

"I—I will be all right as soon as I recover from the shock," she answered. She turned to Longarm and went on, "We must get this woman to a doctor at once. Her wound must be cared for or she may die."

"I'll make you a deal, Miz Roybal," Longarm said. "By rights, I oughta arrest Apache Annie, but you work for the Indian Agency. You take charge of her."

"You will not arrest her?"

Longarm shook his head. "I figure with her and the Apache Kid outa the way there won't be no more trouble."

Calder broke in to say, "Those two and Pawley's bunch, but I can take care of them. And if it makes you feel any better, I've decided to loop the railroad tracks around Frenchman Flat. It'll cost a little more, but the trouble it saves will make it worth my while."

"I sorta figured you'd see it that way," Longarm said. "You tell Sarah and the boys goodbye for me. I figure it's time to close my case. I'll head on back to Denver, because I imagine there's another one waiting for me."

As he walked along the Vegas Wash toward his horse, Longarm took out a long slim cigar from his dwindling supply. He touched a match to it before swinging into his saddle. Trailing a thin line of shimmering smoke behind him, he let his horse set its own gait as he started out of the Vegas Wash and headed for his last look at Frenchman Flat.

Watch for

**LONGARM AND THE ROCKY
MOUNTAIN CHASE**

one hundred and third novel in the bold
LONGARM series from Jove

coming in July!

LONGARM

Explore the exciting Old West with one of the men who made it wild!